AF267470

Other Books by Qapel Doug Duncan

Dharma If You Dare: Living Life with Abandon

Wasteland to Pureland: Reflections on the Path to Awakening (with Catherine Pawasarat)

PSYNAUTS

VOLUME 1
THE SOURCE

QAPEL DOUG DUNCAN

PSYNAUTS
Volume 1: The Source
by Qapel Doug Duncan
First Edition

Planet Dharma
3567 Cockell Road
Fort Steele, British Columbia V0B 1N0
Canada
publishing@planetdharma.com
www.planetdharma.com

ISBN 978-0-9985886-7-4 (paperback)
ISBN 978-0-9985886-8-1 (e-book)

Cover design by Qapel, Catherine Pawasarat, Christopher Lawley & Megumi Yoshida
Interior design by Megumi Yoshida
Author photograph by Kiku Hawkes

Publisher's Note: Qapel Doug Duncan (1949–2024) completed this manuscript before his passing in October 2024. This posthumous publication honours his final creative work and his lifetime of teaching.

Waking up is hard to do.
It takes courage, dedication, and resiliency.
These volumes are dedicated to those who seek, those who find,
and especially to those who help.

THE JOURNAL

There are times when you are just stupid.

There's no way he should have been up on that mountain, Kasya thought, with the sun having just set, clinging to a rock face in a developing blizzard. He was underdressed, ill-prepared, and in no frame of mind to be handling the death-defying activity of mountain climbing. Granted, it wasn't the most challenging of mountains, but a forty-meter drop onto the sheer rock in terrible weather while tired and ill-tempered didn't make for intelligent behavior.

Luckily, the snowstorm was still light, and there was enough moonlight that he managed to spot a small cave. With freezing fingertips and icy toes, Kasya crawled to the little recess that was the entrance to the cave. There was even enough scrub brush around to build a small fire and get him through the night if he rationed it carefully.

He had had the sense to bring his backpack with some candles, matches, water, and a bit of food. It was still early in the fall season, so the temperatures themselves were not life-threatening. Thanks to the scrub, he was able to pass only a mildly uncomfortable night.

As he lit a fire, Kasya reflected on what had gotten him up there in the first place. He had been sitting in a Nepalese teahouse, contemplating his life, and the big question was, "What next?" All of his friends and family, back in his hometown of Minot in North Dakota, were lobbying for him to get a job, start a family, and settle down. And while those prospects had an appeal, Kasya nevertheless felt he was not ready.

He had finished university, although he was probably better suited to a craft, and he'd had a girlfriend in high school he had almost married, except he had gone east to university instead. Then he'd had a girlfriend in college who was vibrant, intelligent, and uninhibited but who didn't want to follow his lifestyle. And then his latest girlfriend might have become "more," but she had committed suicide! This sad event jolted him awake out of complacency. As for work, his research jobs left him dull and his trade job endeavours under-stimulated.

Kasya supposed that many young men and women felt they were missing something in life, and he was no exception. He had tried to do everything the way it was laid out for him from childhood: the standard routine of going to school, graduating, getting a job, getting married, having kids ... and that's about as far as they pointed him. No one really mentioned getting old and dying.

Still, for some reason, Kasya felt something was missing. He couldn't squeeze himself into the box that was expected of him. And that created suffering. It was this suffering that at age eighteen had sent him traveling, looking for alternatives, without any idea that he was looking for alternatives.

So, he had packed his backpack, bought a ticket, and headed off to India, then into the mountains to spend a couple of days hiking in the beautiful fall weather—beautiful, that is, until he was climbing above where it made sense, given his provisions and the weather, and ending up in a developing blizzard. Kasya had wandered off the trails, trusting his smartphone would see him through.

Sitting in a cave in the mountains in a snowstorm, with only a small fire and candle to keep him company, didn't seem so terrible. It's interesting how problems are always framed around the past or the future, he thought, and if he just sat in the moment that is now, then it was a pretty perfect moment.

While he was contemplating the shadows of his body on the wall of the cave, he noticed a pile of rocks in the back corner, arranged in a way that definitely didn't seem random. He went over and took apart the pile of rocks to find a waterproof case and within it a leatherbound journal. Judging by its crisp condition, it hadn't been in the cave very long.

A shiver ran through Kasya's body as he thought about who could've put it there and why. For what possible reason would someone go to the trouble of writing a journal this thick and then leaving it in such a remote and isolated place? Were they still in the area? Would they be coming back? There was no other sign of their presence in the cave.

Sitting by the fire and being careful not to let sparks land on the journal, Kasya slowly opened its pages in case any of them came loose. His excitement mounted as he realized it was going to be easy to read because it was typed and well laid out. Turning to the first page, he read:

Note to reader: This is the chronicle of Avalokana Chen from the planet which Earthlings call Proxima B.

In it, I recount my most recent sojourn on this beautiful planet and my involvement with its inhabitants, predominately Earthlings.

My mission here this time, as always, has been to support the locals to realize their potential not only as Earthly beings but as space-traveling beings as well. We from Proxima B call ourselves Psynauts since the gateway to space–time travel, at least for any great distances, is through the mind (psyche) portal. I have in accordance with Victory Protocol 1 left this record for an auspicious adventurer to discover.

Victory Protocol 1: The greatest value is compassion.

This journal is one of three volumes. The first is to be discovered. The second volume you must receive from a mentor, one of our agents in the field, who will test your suitability. The third volume is really about your journey, different again.

If you're reading this, you are that audacious adventurer or adventurers, and will probably know that this account isn't strictly necessary, as it is part of our procedure to reveal ourselves during our current lifetime on this planet which we do on each visit here. So perhaps you've heard of us but maybe not by that name—Psynauts.

However, it is always good policy to supply multiple references in order to triangulate a point, and this volume is just such a reference.

I am not the only such alien, as you call us, coming to Earth to share our knowledge and experience as well as our expertise in space–time travel with you.

And while it is true that we are not always made very welcome, nor even listened to by most Earthlings, nevertheless, enough of you are paying attention to encourage us to continue our endeavors. And some have even graduated to join our ranks. So, our visits continue, as they have for millennia.

Victory Protocol 2: Only some beings access the methodology to become a Psynaut, although almost all have the capacity.

Lastly, it is only for me to reveal my Earth name so it is contextualized for you. You will most likely know me as Elbud, and if in the unlikely event you haven't heard of me given my very public departure, you might know another of our agents as the current Dalai Lama. Other famous names you might recognize are Lao Tzu, Gautama (called the Buddha), and Jesus (called the Christ), but there are many more. Not all of us are religious figures. Our paths can vary as much as any Earthling's. And of course, there are thousands of us living on this planet even today although very few have chosen the departure method I did. I was in a hurry!

Kasya almost dropped Elbud's book in the fire. Of course, he knew of him. He, Elbud, had emerged from anonymity in the way he had departed from Earth. His—what should it be called?—"evaporation" had made the news worldwide, and people were talking about it everywhere. The speculations were innumerable. They have since died down as no one had a clue, and in any case, not much held people's attention for very long anymore.

Kasya wondered if the journal was legit. Perhaps it was a prank written as a response to Elbud's dramatic departure. He decided to give it the benefit of the doubt for the moment and read on. He didn't have anything else to do in the cave on a stormy night.

But now that Kasya knew that the Dalai Lama, for example, was supposedly a peer of Elbud's, it made sense in a strange way. He knew he wouldn't be looking at the DL, as some called him, the same way ever again.

The fire had dwindled down as he read, and the chill pressed in more bracingly. Kasya added a few more sticks to the fire and cozied up as close to it as he could before returning to his reading.

As for the journal itself, it documents my experience here. How I arrived, how I in-bodied as a human being, how I reconnected to our database on Proxima B through human-level learning triggers (what you Earthlings call conditioning), how I helped disseminate our knowledge (what we call the Victory Protocols), and how I helped train some humans to make "the leap" into what some of you call awakened beings and what we call, as I've said, Psynauts.

Kasya set the book down and stared out into the dark night. The snowstorm continued as he hunkered close to the fire. He had no idea what to do with this information. Whom to tell, whether to publish Elbud's ... what, memoir? He had hidden it away; did that mean Elbud didn't want it widely disseminated?

Kasya decided he would have to think on it. But he grudgingly admitted to himself the worldly thought that he might make some money off this, maybe even some fame. He thought about how he could use the journal to his advantage. Then another thought arose: would Elbud, Avalokana Chen, be especially pleased that someone so motivated found his book? Given Elbud's professed mandate here on Earth, Kasya figured that was what he would have wanted, although Kasya couldn't be really sure since he had found the journal in this forlorn cave.

Kasya looked down at the next part of the journal and felt a bit astonished to read:

Victory Protocol 3: Karma—or activity, the law of cause and effect—is about choices and their predictable results.

Inspired by this Victory Protocol, Kasya ultimately decided to dedicate (most of) the proceeds from this book to a non-profit organization that specialized in spiritual teachings. (Though most people haven't heard of said organization, the curious reader could find it.)

In any case, this night in the mountains in a cave under a starry, late fall sky had certainly turned the wheel of Kasya's life journey in a way he had never envisioned.

Kasya rested his back against the cave wall and stared out into the dark night, deep in thought. He felt like something pivotal was happening that he couldn't name. His eyes closed for a moment ...

Listen

I am what you fear
I interrupt, I take away, I destroy
Tremble, shake, cower
You cannot hide
I ride the night, I come from nowhere, I am behind you

Listen, you might hear my footsteps
Stalking you,
I am death, I am what you have avoided forever
There's no escape
It's only a matter of time

I'm the devourer of dreams and hopes
I'm the wrecker of love and safety
Since you can only cry
Run, little one, run
Can you hear me laughing?

Kasya opened his eyes; he had drifted off. Did he have a dream? He felt a kind of ominous chill that had nothing to do with the dying fire, but he couldn't quite catch what it was. He had the strange feeling he was being watched or followed. He trembled an instant and once more returned to his reading.

PART ONE

Embodying:
Arrival and Childhood

1. Avalokana Chen

This is my report submitted here to the Congress of Proxima B on my mission to what is named locally as Earth, a medium-sized planet inside what they call the solar system. The solar system is part of Shabdkosh Ksheer, what Earthlings call the Milky Way galaxy.

A duplicate copy was left on Earth in accordance with our policy of providing multiple channels of access for humans to the Victory Protocols. As you know, all our various agents in the field do likewise, and mine is but one such account.

As is our custom in these reports, the respective Victory Protocol is presented in the text, while the process of how I remembered or relearned them is explained in the main body of the document, either before or after the relevant protocol.

Of course, the Victory Protocols are always changing as Earthlings evolve over time. So, while none of the inherent wisdom changes, the context evolves, and the "mapping and language" expressing them change also. Thus, this report reflects some of my own additions and refinements.

At this exciting and challenging stage of humanity's growth, the inner realizations are expanded to include outer developments in society at large, resulting in a more integrated understanding. This process is ongoing. For example, what used to be considered "awakening," an inner experience, is now interconnected with science, culture, and community in a more holistic manner.

For the human reader, it must be pointed out that as an arriving "alien," who becomes human by being born on Earth, we too lose contact with the lessons needed to join the field of Psynauts, space–time travelers. Our life experiences, as yours, need to trigger, or refresh, our memories, and the Victory Protocols point out what that lesson was.

Submitted by Avalokana Chen, star date 13.787.000.000.6
Current visitation (birth cycle): 1,008

2. Rebirth

Having completed mission 1,007 a few Earth years earlier, I was preparing for re-entry into Earth manifestation (1,008). As is widely known, when we leave or re-enter Earth as a human being, we faint. At the moment of both death and conception, consciousness goes through a phase change, and in the process, personal memory is wiped clean.

Consciousness at death continues, albeit disembodied, until the relinking karma finds us another body. In that transition period, consciousness returns to Proxima B—home. Some humans have referred to it as the Alaya or, inappropriately named, storehouse consciousness. But this is a mere metaphor.

Victory Protocol 4: The Alaya is part of a supposedly unconsciousness mind wherein impressions of past experiences and karmic actions

are stored. From it, our regular consciousness arises and produces all present and future modes of experience in life. When Psynaut awareness is fully realized, the Alaya consciousness is transformed into the mirror-like wisdom, or perfect discrimination.

For us from Proxima B, however, remembering previous embodiments, as well as the journey in between called the death bardo, is easier, and memory is often quickly retrievable after rebirth as a human.

Victory Protocol 5: There are six bardos, phase changes or in-between states, namely: natural waking, illusory dreaming, altered states, difficult dying, luminous source, and karmic becoming bardo.

There I was in heaven, the death bardo, that in-between place, having the time of my death. I had been floating in a vast, spacious emptiness of calm, peace, and bliss. I liked it. The tranquil quality of darkness sprinkled with twinkling flickers of light was entirely wonderful. It was like being on the ocean, in a desert, or in the prairies on a clear but moonless night that is filled with stars. It was not possible to know whether this was outer space or inner space as there was no sense of a body, no reference point, no way of orienting location, and therefore no measurement of time or space.

The feeling was marvelous and also extremely peaceful; most importantly, "my" mind was at rest. That's something we tend to undervalue no matter which planet or life-form we inhabit. I use "my mind" advisably as there is no ego in this, the luminous source, bardo, just pure consciousness. It is after the fact, in this waking bardo, that "I" and "mine" can be used. In fact, it is only in this waking bardo, the difficult dying bardo, and sometimes the altered states bardo, that the word I or even the experience of "I" is relevant. And in the last case, altered states, the concept of I gets pretty nebulous.

Victory Protocol 6: Everything is impermanent, especially the sense of self.

As I was coursing through space, I saw a light. Two, actually. One was bright and shiny, and the other was more subdued or pastel. They were both appealing. In fact, they were doors. It gets a bit complicated here because from a quantum point of view, I could have gone through both doors simultaneously, but when the body grabs you, you need to choose one. So, I chose the pastel one. Somehow that decision drew me into what would become a male body. Go figure.

Earthlings who practice Buddhism and some of whom live in the Himalayas claim that if the incoming consciousness is attracted to the mother and repels the father, then one is born a boy, and if attracted to the father but repels the mother, one is born a girl. While this gender in-form-ing is true in the physical embodiment (there are some mixed cases), psychologically and emotionally, the gender range extends from one end of the spectrum to the other like a color wheel.

Victory Protocol 7: While reincarnation (building a body) takes time, rebirth (consciousness transference) is instantaneous.

It sounds a bit incestuous. Personally, I think it's a bit unfair (or maybe I'm just greedy), but why can't we beings who incarnate on Earth have two bodies? Who makes that rule? Is there any reason consciousness cannot occupy more than one body at a time? Or maybe it does.

I talked to an evolutionary biologist about this idea of two bodies at once much later in this life, but being a scientist, their imagination was fairly limited—if you can't measure it, it isn't important. Most of them think in terms of matter over mind—primitive! Their measuring system is a self-fulfilling prophecy, fine for certain things, but it leaves actual living in the lurch. Fascinating people, scientists, but not people you'd typically go dancing and partying with, right?

Once embodied and born onto Earth, the consciousness of a human starts to develop what is called an ego, a sense of unique self-identity, around two years of age. This process continues throughout their life, although for most, the sense of self tends to become fixed at around twenty-eight years of age. This has to do with astro-cycles and the energy potential of the life cycle. After twenty-eight, if the life force is not strong enough, most humans stagnate. What determines this is a combination of karma and whether there is dissatisfaction with the ego boundaries.

Victory Protocol 8: From the perspective of the ego, life is a struggle.

And that is what this report will mostly be about, the ego, and its common but unnecessary limitations.

Victory Protocol 9: "Rejoice! Your cruel taskmaster, the ego, exists not."

In other words, the ego is an illusion, but a tricky one. In any case, an illusion doesn't mean it doesn't exist—it just means it doesn't exist the way we think it does!

Transforming these illusions informs my mandate to share the methodology of liberation in the form of Victory Protocols, some of which appear in this report, so that those humans who so desire can enroll in the league of Psynauts. The examples of life experiences herein contained are to demonstrate my path, as a human being, to that purpose.

"I" had just doffed one ego and had not yet donned another. You can see the circular nature of this whole process. It's really like a dream, the ego. When you're in it, the dream seems so real, and when you wake up, poof—where did it go? In fact, most of us have been here before, although memory is a fickle creature on that score. Before I showed up in space this time, I'd lived and died here on Earth many times. What can you do … karma is inexorable!

And that's what makes me, and you as well, an alien, a person from somewhere else. We from Proxima B prefer to call ourselves Psynauts, mind travelers, because it sounds nicer than alien. We forget to treat the ego like clothes to be put on or thrown off at will. Naked is nice!

Unbeknownst to me, my ability to know where I was and what was going on indicated I had inhabited this thing called the body. And like all bodies, there are rules, and one of them is that they go from one place to another, in this case, from womb to tomb via the intense processes of life.

Looking at life like a detective novel, working backwards from the result, this body, soon to be a corpse, to the triggering event, getting conceived, which is a result of having died, is truly a mystery … a real whodunit.

3. Womb Time

Once I had arrived in a womb, there followed a forty-week building project. That project was my body. Describing life in the womb will be brief as most of it is pre-self-conscious. So, if you are curious about your own birth process, I recommend you sit yourself down alone somewhere and see what you can remember. It may take a while. Take my advice and try to remember where you came from before you traveled down that tunnel of birth because it is the origin of everything that comes later, namely "you," and in large measure molds what you will become.

Victory Protocol 10: Life's events gravitate towards and reinforce events of the womb shaping.

Those forty weeks seem vague to me now. It was dark in the womb, but there was a dim light, and I could hear some sounds, somewhat similar to putting your head underwater in the bathtub and then humming. There's a muted heartbeat feel to it, probably reminiscent of our mother's. Being in the womb was also like being in the ocean; there were currents and tides, feelings of warm and cold, and curiously, there were smells, mostly sweet. You can't say an ocean has feelings, but insofar as it does, it was generally very pleasant. Perhaps that's where meditators came up with the term ocean seal samadhi, absorption. The Buddhists call it jhana.

Victory Protocol 11: Different levels of meditative absorption are graduated steps for "liftoff" into the realm of Psynaut access. Typically, there are nine such steps.

Sure, there were disturbances, rumblings, pressures, and chemical "washings." When all was calm and things were quiet, in both my inner environment and the outer world, it was extremely comfortable. But when, for instance, the two people I'd learn to call mother and father were having arguments and conflicting emotions, it caused some turmoil in my little cave in the form of stomach disturbances and nausea.

But my principal memory was motion. It was like being in a sleeper car on the railroad in my own little room, speeding through the countryside, especially at night, the train swaying, the clickety-clack of the wheels on the rails. It was very soothing, riding around in my own private womb. (Private in my case, anyway.) But you can't stay there forever, or anywhere else for that matter—after all, we are all orphans and homeless in the end. The contractions were the alarm clock.

Victory Protocol 12: Freedom is to abide where there is no abiding.

Generally, though it was heaven, maybe it's where we get that idea of heaven from: the early days of womb bliss. Perhaps that's also where we get our idea of the Garden of Eden. And maybe the idea of being thrown out of Eden reflects our birth process and the sense of impermanence.

Victory Protocol 13: Religion is literal; spirituality is metaphorical.

From vast open space, to the closed space vehicle of the womb, to birth, is also impermanent. I was about to find out just how impermanent. My cozy world was about to be interrupted. Paradise lost.

4. Birth

Like many interruptions, this one started slow—in fact, it was almost unnoticeable. Why do we think there won't be, or shouldn't be, interruptions?

I felt a rumble. It was gentle at first—little more than a nudge—but enough to get my attention. The disturbance grew, and the interruptions kept coming. They became more regular. The disturbances gradually grew more intense until finally they were a full onslaught. It was as if I had been cradled in the heaven of space, and then I was catapulted toward hell. This was a good introduction to the journey through life in this world upon which I was about to embark. Heaven or hell, or both? They can switch so quickly. And it teaches you that life is a struggle.

Victory Protocol 14: Four Psynaut realizations: life is a struggle, caused by attachment, release is possible, and there is a methodology of release.

The onslaught sucked me into a vortex-like funnel that consumed me as it got narrower and narrower. Did I tell you it was intense? Goddamn, it was intense! I say goddamn because no self-respecting God would have anything to do with it. But then, it was impermanent, although I didn't know it at the time. In fact, I had no idea that there was such a thing as time or impermanence or heaven or hell. It just was. It was terrifying to have no idea what was going on.

Victory Protocol 15: Four great fears: annihilation, abandonment, mental breakdown (going "crazy"), and being "evil" (the shadow manifesting).

What was hell like, you ask? Imagine being crushed by a mountain into tangled pieces of dust, imagine being burned alive with your skin peeling off and bubbling, imagine being torn apart by wild animals and devoured, imagine being smothered and suffocated, imagine being unable to breathe but somehow managing to catch a breath, imagine being poisoned with the toxic waste from a million years of human chemical dumps.

But perhaps the most fearsome thing was the sensation of falling. Falling, falling, falling from nowhere to nowhere. That was different to being in space where there was no sense of falling even if there was a subtle sensation of movement. The falling seemed to go on forever. I really didn't expect to survive it. Did I mention feeling crushed to pieces? Right at the end, I felt like I had been garroted. I was choking and gasping for air with this cord wrapped around my neck, but somehow, someone managed to get it untangled. I could breathe.

And then, PLOP! Here I was, a new baby on Earth, one of billions of people, not yet ready to meet what was happening but with no choice but to do so. My first impressions were not all that wonderful. It was bright, noisy, and cold. I was handed around like a baseball trading card, and everyone had something to say about me. Have you ever found that when life brings a major change, you are never really ready to meet it, but somehow it works out anyway?

Birth is a bitch. Sure, some women and mothers will tell you that giving birth is a magical experience, probably because it is their kundalini experience, with forty weeks of practice. But that's unfair from the point of view of the child because the mother knows more of what's going on while the baby doesn't.

Victory Protocol 16: Our body rides on the energy (chi, wind) contained therein when consciousness embodies. Its movement through the organism's energy centers is called kundalini.

From my experience, I had no idea what was happening. In spite of the number of times I've done it, I wouldn't want to go through it again, at least without knowing it would end. I really need to try to remember that I'm on some sort of horror carnival ride: while I can yell and scream, metaphorically, I will eventually get off and walk away, also metaphorically. At least most of the time, with most of the time, with modern medicine to help if needed.

Victory Protocol 17: The birth process initiates all the qualities and strengths we will need to meet life successfully. Interfering with that process creates an enormous struggle. (Unnecessary caesareans are a very bad idea for this reason.)

In my new baby boy body, I couldn't understand why everybody was wearing white, but from my perspective at this time, it was just one of the many crazy things people got up to on this planet.

They handed me off to this woman, who turned out to be my mother, and to whom I would be attached in various degrees over the next decade or so. My initial reaction to being in her arms after the journey I had just been through was a huge relief. Granted, it would not always be so, especially after I turned two, but it evened out later once we had established our boundaries. It seemed I always had to be clearer about boundaries than she did, but I've come to learn since that this is universal for humans.

I was just beginning to settle in her arms when someone dressed in white came and took me away again. They put me in a room with a bunch of other strange creatures. I couldn't figure out for the life of me why. They were a bunch of small mummies surrounded by a bevy of white-clad women called nurses. Some of those bundles cried, cooed, and others just lay there. I took the last strategy, waiting to see what was going to happen next. After all, it had been a busy twenty-four hours, and I could use the break.

In rather short order, from the adult's perspective, I was loaded up in a car and driven off once more to a new environment. I was getting the idea that this might become rather commonplace, moving around from location to location. It was disconcerting at this stage, but I got accustomed to it over time. But—and I know this is not news to any-one—change came as a surprise. As we saw in Victory Protocol 6, everything is impermanent except impermanence.

For this life cycle, 1,008, my initial conclusion was that deep space was fantastic, the forty weeks in the womb-cave were excellent too, and that half day of terror and violence in the chamber of death before I arrived in the New World was bearable ... after the fact! I'd arrived in my own new Jerusalem.

My cursory assessment at this new world in those early days was "What a buzz." I had a feeling I was going to be very busy for a long time, and that's exactly how it turned out.

5. Getting Landed

The first few years were incredibly busy, mostly focused on the development of a self, an ego identity. I've had a few jobs during my lifetime on Earth, but this baby business was seriously full-time. Granted, I slept a lot, and I didn't have to change my diapers or do the dishes or even brush my teeth, but nevertheless, they kept me going all the time.

Learning to talk and walk was not exactly a piece of cake. Once, I toddled off the front stoop and fell two or three feet to the ground. Luckily, I landed on the grass, which had a sleeping dog in it. I tried to convince Daisy, as they called her, that it really wasn't my fault I landed on her, as I hadn't yet earned my walking license, but she took off in such a hurry that I couldn't make myself clear. Besides which she didn't speak English, and my "dog tongue," which I thought was pretty good, didn't impress her.

It's funny that no one seems to get traumatized over learning to walk! You would think all that falling down and getting bumped and scraped would be cause for years of therapy. Maybe trauma is conjoined with a sense of self which we don't have yet at that age. Maybe not clinging to a self prevents trauma?

Victory Protocol 9.1 (variant): The sense of a fixed, permanent, independent self is an illusion.

One of the great things about being that age is what you can sleep on. I liked sleeping on Daisy. She was warm and cuddly, and she put up with almost anything. I didn't really like my crib, but I did have a dangling mobile that was really fun to watch and, despite all the interruptions, gave me some great states. Cutting my teeth sucked, but I loved iodine—what a great taste. This theme of good states and bad states is universal for humans on Earth, at least until the stage of Psynaut.

Victory Protocol 18: Life is a cycle of transformations based on attachments and/or aversions.

And who came up with this language? To make just the right sound, you have to contort your mouth into so many shapes, and then the tongue gets in the way. I finally learned enough of the language just in time for the woman in my life to decide there were a lot of rules. I don't know whether those things generally happen in tandem, but as soon as I could put two words together, my self-expression became subject to more constraints. I guess my first words were "ma" and "da," but I'm pretty sure my third word was "no," or at least that's what my mother told me. But I have a sneaking suspicion she was biased.

My mother said I was the perfect baby until I was two, which, coincidentally, was when I learned to talk. At around age two, the ego develops enough for the baby to self-recognize, which by implication means that "mother" becomes "other." The great abandonment!

Victory Protocol 8.1 (variant): Being separated from what is desired is suffering. Being conjoined with what is not desired is also suffering.

I guess that's when the battle of the wills, and the resulting rage, set in. No, we are not in control, and we are totally dependent. Not a great combo! Are human beings big arguers as adults just to establish our independence from mother, or is it compensation for our fear of being abandoned? Babies cry to get what they want, and adults have arguments or maybe just go shopping and watch TV. (Big industries, such as pharmaceuticals, have made a fortune off these patterns.)

Victory Protocol 19: Emotional states are determined by the human evaluating system known as feelings. Feelings are conditioned by association with what is considered pleasant, unpleasant, or neutral. These two are programmed by previous karma (how the initial contact was delivered and received).

I once heard that the average person is born young and grows old, but mystics are born old (old souls) and grow young. It seems our bodily sensations come first, and then our feelings are built around how we evaluate (like or dislike) those sensations. After this, we plan and scheme, using our intellect to manage it all, avoiding what we've learned is unpleasant and seeking what we've identified as pleasant.

A mystic is born knowing this already and downloads the programming, returning more and more to the pure perception of sensation. This idea of programming, conditioning, introduces us to some ways humans learn when young, notably:

- boundaries such as ownership (from breasts to food and toys);
- species (humans and everything else);
- chain of command (who gets to decide—mother and father to siblings and beyond);
- safety (what you can risk);
- independence (how far you can go and still feel safe);
- relationships (from siblings to girls and boys, school and jobs);
- training (fitting in, getting along, and skills) and;
- consciousness (waking and dreaming).

I was about to learn the rules of the game.

6. Boundaries

OWNERSHIP: FROM BREASTS TO MILK AND MONEY

I did have one great complaint from those early days: who gets to decide whose breasts they are, anyway? In my opinion, while they weren't exactly mine, nevertheless, I felt I had some proprietary, capitalist-type ownership or right to them. After all, mother tells you she will do anything for you, and she loves you totally, but it seemed to me then that the breasts should've been included in my dietary schedule. Alas, they were off limits for me, so it's not really my fault that I followed those things around for all my adult life on the off chance … well, you know.

Bottle-feeding was common in those days (the 1950s). Many mothers besides my own didn't breastfeed their young, and one of my mentors from Proxima B speculated years later, when I was doing some advanced training with him, that it might be a contributing cause, along with drugged births, to my generation's obsession with loose sex, seeking more contact, and drug use.

I was somewhat compensated by my father (who never played a lot of sports, having grown up in the Great Depression) who liked to throw me up in the air and catch me. I was ecstatic about this. The free-fall reminded me of being out in space earlier in my journey just before becoming a human being. The feeling of weightlessness—and when he did it outside in the sun, the feeling of the light—was enormously pleasant compared to going down through that cramped tunnel to Earth.

The early years were a crash course in ownership. I never really got the idea of ownership very well since everything starts somewhere and ends up going somewhere else. We only have things for a short time. I guess you could say you own them while they are passing through your hands.

When I was around four years old, I used to walk up and down the street in my neighborhood. In those days, the milkman used to deliver to people's front doors, and leave the milk and the change on the stoop. I figured that meant it was up for grabs. So, with my red blanket over my shoulder, I would wander down the street, drinking the milk and pocketing the change. Occasionally being observed in this act by our neighbors, I would be invited in for breakfast. In this way, I'd sometimes eat two or three breakfasts a day.

It turned out to be good practice for years later when I was a monk for a while, embracing higher-level training. We monks wandered door-to-door, offering people the opportunity to feed us in exchange for our prayers on their behalf. That brings me to:

Victory Protocol 20: Generosity is a fundamental element (1 of 6 virtues, more on these later) of a Psynaut's realization. To be generous, we must trust and surrender to the reality that we have enough and can share.

Curiously, the red blanket that I carried on my milk rounds was not unlike the colors of my monk's robe and went everywhere with me until I outgrew it. A few years later, my mother bought me a red jacket that

I insisted on having, but I lost it. Expecting my mother to be upset, I was surprised when she was relieved; she had had a dream that I died in my red jacket.

My mother was a psychic and had a great many of those experiences, some of which were documentable. This talent, possessed by my mother, her two sisters, and their mother, wasn't considered unusual in my family; we thought it was normal. Her psychic abilities were an initial indicator for me that our world was much larger than what appeared to our senses. In another era, they might have been deemed witches or shamans. While they never had the mapping systems that we Psynauts use, their experiences were similar. But more on this later.

Victory Protocol 21: The so-called Psychic powers that arise occasionally, as needed in a Psynaut's work, are not for show.

SPECIES: HUMANS AND ANIMALS

I've always loved animals and nature. When I was about four years old, my parents decided to take a holiday with my brother and sister, leaving me behind with family friends, but they were no friends of mine. That didn't mean I didn't like them; I simply had no idea who they were. I was just getting used to the aliens called my parents and wasn't prepared for a new set so soon.

Luckily, they had a labrador retriever, and it seemed a good strategy to eat my meals underneath the table with the dog. I particularly liked his method of going straight to the bowl and not bothering with the hands—granted, he didn't have any—but I never mastered the technique as well as he did. Nevertheless, we had a fantastic time and got along famously.

I don't remember the people much, but they must've been pretty easygoing to let a four-year-old sit under the table and eat his food from a bowl like a dog. Of course, I might also have been quite a handful, and it would have been a good way to shut me up. In any case, it's a fond memory.

Victory Protocol 22: Treat all life with respect and disturb it as little as possible.

CHAIN OF COMMAND: WHO GETS TO DECIDE

I started to learn about control from my older sister who was ten years older than me. One of these lessons revolved around what would become food prejudices. These biases often creep into our lives and can last a lifetime if we can't see them.

On this occasion, I was in a high chair, perhaps two or three years of age. She was assigned the task of giving me my egg for lunch as my mother was going to be away. Carol dutifully tried to get this egg down my throat, and I did everything I could to avoid it—the egg was rotten, and my sister wasn't old enough to notice. The war of the wills was on, and while she had size, strength, and mobility, I had great motivation in rejecting the sulphur-smelling egg. I don't remember the outcome, but I have a feeling it was some kind of stalemate. In any case, I couldn't eat hard-boiled eggs again until many years later because every time I saw an egg, I would get nauseous. I guess this is how humans develop sensitivities and traumas.

Many years later, in my twenties, I was traveling in India and had found myself in the Khyber Pass for a couple of days with nothing to eat except hard-boiled eggs. Hunger drove me to get over myself, and the problem with hard-boiled eggs disappeared. But every time I ate them, the memory would resurface.

I harbored no resentment towards my sister for a couple of reasons. One, I don't think she knew the egg was rotten, and two, she felt she was only doing what she had to: control me, as represented by the power structure and her need to win approval as well as avoid reprimand from our mother. For my part, I had tried to control her by spitting it out. In this sense, all battles of aggression or dominance are about control.

Victory Protocol 8.2/18.1 (variants): Suffering occurs because of attachments or aversions generally rooted in greed, hatred, or delusion.

INDEPENDENCE: HOW FAR YOU CAN GO AND STILL FEEL SAFE

I remember the awesome adventure called "the street," from when I was a little bit older. It was an awesome thing because I was not allowed to cross it. The instructions were clear: I could go up to the sidewalk, and I could walk up and down it, but I could not venture out beyond the curb. And like every self-respecting young child, I of course walked across the street before permission was granted.

Victory Protocol 23: We never feel we're ready for the challenge that comes next, but if it is arising, we most probably are.

I remember the feeling like it was yesterday, and from my world, it was ... I mean, given that I traveled across the solar system to get here, what is the street, after all? Anyway, when I finally crossed it, I was ecstatic. I felt like Caesar crossing the Rubicon, Moses crossing the Red Sea, Jesus getting tired of sitting in the tomb ... you get the idea.

It was becoming more and more clear to me that life was an ongoing series of challenges; walking, talking, streets, knives and forks, toilet training, on it went. And then there were girls and getting lost. These are not necessarily in order of importance but rather in terms of temporality, so I'll talk about wanderlust first.

I was born a wanderer. I was always running away from home. Actually, this was my parent's perspective; from my perspective, I was just going where I was going. Children can often dwell in ecstasy as it is our original nature. This is reflected in:

Victory Protocol 24: The natural state for a human being is bliss, clarity, and non-clinging.

As an example of the wandering spirit, once I ran away to the farm when I was about five years old. My aunt and uncle lived in a small farmhouse, tiny by today's standards. There was a family gathering that day, so there were lots of kids around. My aunt generously allowed all of us to stay over for the night, but my mother figured my aunt already had her hands full with so many rambunctious children and insisted I return home.

I had a different opinion, so very early the next morning, I packed my most essential possessions as I got ready to return to the farm. I took my balsa wood airplane, my marbles, and my cod liver oil. I left before my parents were up and headed out of town. Saskatoon at that time was not a big place and still isn't, but for a four-year-old, it was an effort. I got a lift from a nice lady to the edge of town (to her dying day, my mother couldn't fathom who would drop a four-year-old off at the edge of town). I started walking south towards the farm, about five miles away, and was halfway there when a police car pulled up beside me.

The officer asked me if I was Elbud, and I remember answering, "Why?" As far as cops go, he was pretty smart, and he said, "Well, if you are Elbud, you could ride in the police car with me and wear my hat." Shit, life is full of choices. The farm and all those kids to play with, or the cop car and a hat … what would you do? I opted for the cop car.

Looking back, I think I weighed up a known pleasure, being at the farm, with an unknown potential pleasure, riding in the cop car, and opted for the latter. On the return to town, I did in fact get to wear his hat, which was way too big for me, so I couldn't really see where we were going. But I got an unexpected bonus: when I asked him to turn on his siren for me, he complied for a few seconds.

He safely returned me to my mother's arms, and while she seemed relieved, it did not prevent her from scolding me severely. Unfortunately for her, the episode didn't really change my behavior, but fortunately for me, it helped instill a lifelong love of travel.

Another occasion of my wanderlust that occurred at about the same time as the farm journey was when I decided to visit my father at work. I knew the general direction, so I headed off walking the fifteen or so blocks. I'd been there in the car before, so I thought I could just retrace the route. But walking is different from riding in the car. After walking most of the distance, I ended up at a traffic light. This was a new experience, and as I was standing there thinking about my next move, a police officer walked up to me and asked, "Little boy, are you lost?" You've got to love small towns. In spite of how it sounds, and how I turned out later, I wasn't being a smartass when I replied, "No, sir, I'm not lost, I just don't know where I am."

Victory Principle 25 stresses the unknowing and unknowable nature of reality: We live in a mystery and only see what pops out of the void into our world.

He bundled me up in the police car, and we proceeded to drive all over town, looking for my house. When we finally found it, my mother was standing on the sidewalk, searching for me again. Eventually we would all get to know each other well enough to the point where the town policemen would just drive me straight home and say, "Here he is, Mrs. D." While the police were not visibly entertained, I did have a sense they kind of enjoyed it. My wandering off became a shared experience in the neighborhood.

One of the qualities of a Buddhist monk is homelessness. Perhaps I was preparing for my future, or maybe it was from a past life, and I was just acting true to form?

RELATIONSHIPS: FROM GIRLS TO SIBLINGS

As humans get older, gender starts to make itself known, and the first hints of gender difference stir. In my case, I was about to discover girls, who were to be a major theme in my life.

One such memory, when I was about four, involved the girl who lived across the street. She and I were playing between two houses when she proposed the idea that we take our clothes off. I saw no reason not to comply. As we were standing there, stark naked, my mother came around one corner of the house, and her mother came around from the other corner of the house, trapping us in the middle. They were trying to find out where we had disappeared to.

What is interesting about this, since probably almost every kid has had a similar experience, is that while being naked with the little girl was fun, we both felt "caught" as if what we were doing was somehow wrong. What I didn't really understand for a long time is how a four-year-old could incorporate their parent's issues around nudity and sexuality at such a young age. I thought about this over the years and came up with two ideas about it.

The first idea is about some sort of past life memory. After millions of years of selfish genes and another 10,000 years of even more possessive agriculture, the values associated with these, such as ownership, inheritance, and power, have come to instill in us "inherited" feelings of guilt and shame when our activities are not sanctioned by society. Granted, the little girl and I were not about to make babies, but conditioning runs deep.

The second idea, which is related, is that I picked up the "guilt" or "shame" from my parents through osmosis … all those mirror neurons bouncing around, telling us to feel what others are feeling. On that note, as my friend Charles Cooley said, "I'm not who I think I am and perhaps not who you think I am, but maybe I am what I think that you think I am." This brings us to:

Victory Protocol 26: We are all an interweaving of interdependent patterns, and those patterns trigger a sense of being or person we call "me."

It was about then that my siblings started to dawn on my consciousness.

TRAINING: FITTING IN AND GETTING ALONG

I was the third born, so my mother had had some practice with children by the time I appeared. The birth order is a bit of a crapshoot. For instance, if you're born third, your parents have already had some practice with your siblings. They've learned a few things, worked out the kinks; they tend to be more laissez-faire. And as the third, you can get away with more on the basis of "divide and conquer." In my case, as the youngest, I also had two self-centered egos to go through in order to get what I wanted. And unfortunately, older siblings tend to want the same stuff you do, not to mention they are bigger, stronger, and more skilled.

I felt I was getting the results of my parents' ongoing on-the-job training. Having untrained people in charge of raising, managing, supervising, and caring for me and then to be let loose in the world didn't portend great results. I don't know about you, but I'd like my doctor, pilot, parent, and romantic partner to have had some training and experience.

In any case, birth order is a mixed bag, as is marriage, but for some reason, we keep getting born and married (or its equivalent). Perhaps it's the abandonment issue again? As social animals, humans have used this asset of socialization to survive and dominate the planet, not always to its benefit. Being alone can be a very dangerous and threatening experience. Most of us just make it up as we go.

Victory Protocol 27: To realize our Psynaut potential requires training.

Saints and hermits like to be alone but typically not for very long. Perhaps it's learning to be okay with being alone that allows one to access those early days of spacious blissful unity that lie behind the personality and ego. This was true in my experience, which we will see in the journey ahead: my transition from human back to Psynaut.

During this transition to remembering I was a Psynaut, I was reintroduced to the Victory Protocols. Every visit to Earth requires this remembering, or retraining, because the human envelope is very dense. The training is the technology by which a person can transition from being a human to becoming a Psynaut even if it is their first time, that is, if they haven't yet been to Proxima B.

The Protocols are a combination of a change in views or understanding, as well as a map that includes methodology. The numbers assigned to the protocols refer to where they sit in the schedule. Some "Nauts" will alter the numbers and their order, but in general, that's not important once you have a grasp of their purpose and application. So, starting from first principles:

Victory Protocol 2.1 (variant): Every human being has the potential to access and integrate their Psynaut nature. This has been called Buddha nature, Christ consciousness, God mind, and so on by humans learning the way.

I realized that there was far more to us than just being human, being born, working, propagating, chasing appetites, and dying. Christ and Buddha are the two Psynauts most humans know of. These two are considered special, and the common belief is that the average person isn't. But what was true for Christ and Buddha is, potentially, true for almost everyone. Becoming a Psynaut is truly challenging work, but it is a human birthright!

If I expect others to have training, I cannot exempt myself. Not all of us look forward to training of any kind, given the implication of hard work involved. Curiously, that's what my mother told me: "You need training."

Almost as soon as I could walk and talk, the lessons were on. Kids are wild and uncontrolled, so in order to get along with others and fit in to our communities, we need to be able to cooperate and contribute, ergo, get trained—from how to go to the bathroom and to how to use a knife and fork, to how to get along with those troublesome other egos around us. I feel my training could've been better managed however, and funnily enough, everybody I know says the same thing about their training.

Unfortunately, as adults, we see training as discipline or correction, rather than its original intent which is "learning," especially when it extends beyond career and moves into social behavior. Early childhood training revolves around social behavior.

The anecdotes in this narrative reflect the unconscious and conditioned nature of that training which became so habitual that it melted into the subconscious. So, when a new kind of training is required in order to embrace our Psynaut nature, we often rebel.

Victory Protocol 28: If you don't rebel, you probably don't meet the Victory Protocols. If you keep rebelling, you probably won't learn them.

CONSCIOUSNESS: DREAMS AND NOTHING

There are many different realms we, our consciousness, can abide in: the waking realm, the dream realm, and the altered states realm, to name a few. I've mentioned these bardos before. I have one last story about my early years which has served me well, both on and off this planet, in terms of how consciousness manifests.

I hadn't yet gotten accustomed to the rapidity of impermanence and the fluid movement of realms here on Earth when I had a startling nightmare. When I was about four, I had a dream that a man dressed in black leather, riding a black motorcycle with a black sidecar, came to the front door. He took my parents, put them in the sidecar, and drove away, leaving me all alone …

Darkness

I am the dream
I make promises, and I take them away
I am the nightmare, I am the curse
I am the disappointment of lost causes
I am annihilation
I am abandonment
You can't be saved, little one

I make you the orphan
I render you homeless
Your scrambling to try and make it safe
Amuses me
Shiver, quake, and shake
Prayers are not enough

I had this recurring nightmare over and over every night for weeks until the day we moved, and I found myself in a new bedroom in a new house with my parents and siblings. Somehow, my four-year-old self had sensed the move as a threat, not knowing if he was going to be left behind. Of course, at that age, I had no idea about houses and moving. We know more than we think we know, and we know it in ways we never know how we know it.

Victory Protocol 4.1 (variant): The Ālayavijñāna, substratum consciousness, refers to the so-called unconscious level of experience. It also includes where our habits are maintained and where they transform. But it is transpersonal; it is everyone's unconscious. It is the essence of consciousness itself.

Sometimes this storehouse, or library, of collective consciousness is observed by what could be called "the witness." The witness is that part of ourselves that observes what we say, do, and think, but doesn't interact. Nevertheless, there is no actual witness because there is no "thing" to be a witness too.

Victory Protocol 29: The Mind is nowhere to be found. There is only non-clinging. The mind is transient and insubstantial. There is knowing but no one to know it.

Humans like to have everything figured out, but in the end, we live in a mystery, moving from unknown to unknown, trying to fake it till we make it, not realizing that the whole story while yet unwritten has nevertheless been written by unseen hands of an unformed energy that some like to call "God(s)," or maybe "evolution." It's pretty cool, but the ego doesn't like it. It's difficult for egos to accept that they exist on the basis of self-referencing and that if we just allowed ourselves to rest in the moment, all would be revealed.

7. Departures and New Beginnings

The previous chapters have summarized the first stage of my life adventure here on planet Earth. I still hadn't recalled my origins on Proxima B, nor that I was a Psynaut, nor the Victory Protocols, but the flow of life experience was accumulating to trigger the question that was not yet asked. For that to happen, I'd need to develop an ego identity and incorporate some more defined values that were delivered by my parents and society—precursors to an even later development of one's worldviews and what we take faith in.

From the perspective of the Victory Protocols, the foregoing was to show how we are all space beings who are then formed by our womb experiences and conditioned by early life experiences as humans. The emerging self coagulates around blissful and painful moments, and our training shapes how we meet life's events. It also introduces the idea that our mind is much bigger than what we see and think, as in the nightmare experience from the previous chapter.

The question not yet asked is: what draws or compels us to reach out, investigate, and probe the unknown? Many beings across time and space have asked it in various ways. For me, it came down to:

"What is this 'happening' I'm experiencing?"

Next up for me was a new house, a new neighborhood, starting school, and Elbud version 2.0.

***

Kasya sat back, rubbing his eyes. He couldn't believe what he was reading. It was shaking him to his core. All his life, he'd been searching for something, feeling there was something more. And now, of all things, that "something more" had to include an alien! Wasn't that just in movies?

Sitting in this Himalayan cave in the middle of the night, he wondered about choices and directions. Did he actually have a choice? Was he destined to tread the uncommon path? The journal of Avalokana Chen, Elbud, roused his curiosity and provided a motivation that he could embrace—could he become a Psynaut? And what did that mean? How did one become a Psynaut, not to mention reincarnate? For that matter, why should he bother?

As the storm continued, Kasya reflected on the death of his latest girlfriend. She had jumped off a building the previous year. She might have become his chance at something more serious, but the rug had been pulled out from under his sense of permanence and reliability in life goals. He felt everything was out of control, uncertain.

He'd been on a therapy course that involved first meeting your aspiration for growth and development, whatever that meant, and then fulfilling that aspiration by overcoming what was called the demon of resistance. The demon was all the fears and attachments that stand in our way to becoming more than we are. He'd read, "If you want to become more than you are, you have to become what you're not."

When Kasya thought about what was pushing him on the search for more, he sensed there was much negativity involved. He wasn't satisfied with this life, and that was painful to realize. Even worse, he didn't know what to do about it. And of course, Susan had died. How could an ordinary life satisfy him if at any moment it could disappear like Susan?

At first glance, his motivation was to get out of the pain. If the best way to do so was to become a Psynaut, then he figured it would also help his friends and family. After all, Kasya felt that in spite of their claims, they sure didn't look happy. Judging by how they behaved, it seemed they were in more pain than he was but couldn't see it for themselves. This, in part, pushed him to rebel against the standard operating procedure of normal life—so he had gone hiking in the mountains of India in the interim.

Could he do this, did he really want to? Kasya decided to keep on reading, as long as he was caught in this Himalayan cave.

But, aliens! Were they really among us? Was it perhaps a metaphor? And if so, what about Proxima B and the enclave of its inhabitants? Not to mention "reincarnation" was surely a jest?

Gazing off into the dark, blustery night, Kasya wondered what organized religion and capitalist powers made of Psynauts. As his mind drifted, he sensed something ... just ... outside ... his ... r ... e ... a ... c ...h ...

Blindness

I am darkness and the unknown
You cannot see me
I walk just behind you always
Can you hear my footsteps?
No, I am not your friend
You call me the enemy
The demon, the devil, the evil one
How little you know should scare you
But you are drugged
And I will devour you for it

Kasya sensed something just beyond the threshold of his awareness. It was like he'd had this feeling before but couldn't quite place it. He felt anxious for some reason, but it was hard to say why. Shaking off the feeling, Kasya picked up the journal and continued reading.

PART TWO

The Emerging Self: Coming of Age

8. Orientation

I have spent time here on the early years since they're so formative for us all. Like my old friend Aristotle used to say when I bothered him with questions in earlier appearances on Earth, "Give me a child until he is seven, and I will show you the man." I don't think this lets girls off the hook, by the way. In fact, girls may not even get that much time, since they tend to develop faster. Maybe they only get until five before the woman is obvious?

Those early years were interesting. I found out how to live in a body, I got my feet working, and my hands got pretty good at manipulating things since my mother was always saying, "Elbud, put that down." I could also make a full sentence, and sometimes it even made sense. Generally, I could be on my own without walking off a cliff, burning down the house, or causing some other disaster that I'm sure my parents thought was going to happen if they weren't around to supervise.

It's hard to say exactly when the trouble started, but I believe it was around age two. With the arising of an ego, so arises trouble. It's a strange process that you first need an ego before you can even know what trouble is. And then it takes years to realize that your ego is relative; it lives in an ocean of other egos. And it takes even more time to realize that they aren't as interested in you as you are. Curiously, this is what makes many humans want to transcend the ego: to get out of the trap of an isolating and illusory perception of reality.

Victory Protocol 8.3 (variant): Life is a struggle.

We don't know who discovered water, but we know it wasn't a fish. Maybe a dolphin. The ego is our dolphin. The fact is that most people only do step one, get an ego, and ignore step two, transcend it. The Victory Protocols are trying to encourage the move to step two, what we call liberation. To do so doesn't dawn on anyone seriously, myself included, until we are much older.

For some, the idea of liberation from the ego arises in their late teens, others in their twenties, some near the end of their lives, and for some not at all, at least this time around. The funny thing about transcendence is that it isn't understandable from an ego's point of view. Most of us think we're ordinary—okay, we probably think we're a little extra—yet more intelligent, more charming, more humorous, more loving, and so on than we really are. But this doesn't describe the trouble we get into when under the influence of the ego. The ego is a necessary, amazing, and wonderful tool, but it is a terrible master.

In essence, this is what got me moving. From where I was sitting, I was just a kid like any other. In retrospect, it was as if I was a caterpillar destined to be a butterfly—this in itself isn't special; metamorphosis is an entirely natural process. Everyone's destined to be a free-flying butterfly, which we can sometimes forget because many of us get distracted as caterpillars for far too long while others keep bouncing against a net not initially of their own design.

Victory Protocol 27.1 (variant): The process of graduating from human to Psynaut involves training that proceeds in steps.

I was in trouble. That's why they probably call them the terrible twos. I suppose we could call them the troubled twos. It's the time when we start to differentiate, or individuate, from our parents. But it probably takes until five or seven, à la Aristotle, before we start to show what we, our ego, is going to look like. Part of us needs to fit in and go along, belong, and another part needs to go its own way to self-actualize or better, to transcend. Curiously, it is the transcending of self that really allows us to cooperate.

It was the Buddha, I think, who said, "All things are done for the sake of self," so I suppose that applies to both going along as well as not going along.

Victory Protocol 9.2 (variant): All things are done for the sake of self.

As one of my teachers said many years later, "I don't trust a student who doesn't rebel," meaning that a certain amount of independence is necessary to make a change. That's the thing about trouble: it can lead to change, or it can just be more trouble. It took me many years to see the difference. Children don't see the trouble they're in until after the fact. We have to be taught what it is, and hopefully, we learn something along the way. The developing self has a lot to learn.

However, my teacher could also have said, that once you've seen the prison and opened the door, to keep rebelling is to just stand in the doorway and complain. Eventually, we must rebel against rebelling if we want to build something new and amazing.

9. School

While parents are at first our biggest influence, once we are about five years old, our world expands exponentially with institutionalized education.

I remember the first day of school. My mother walked me there because it was far, holding my hand the entire way. I think there is a space–time warp surrounding planet Earth because when I retraced my steps some years later, the distance had magically shrunk, and the time it took to get there had also shrunk. I've talked to many humans over the years, and I have found this to be consistent regardless of race, color, creed, or gender: everyone seems to have experienced this space–time warp, but most of us seem to ignore it from day to day.

Victory Protocol 30: What measure measures the measurer's measure?

When we got to the school, my mother was surprised that, as we got within range of other kids, I insisted she let go of my hand. I put a brave face on, but given the choice between traveling through interstellar space at warp speed and entering a schoolyard for the first time, as a five-year-old, I'd choose space every time. The symbiotic relationship has to end sometime for us to grow up.

Victory Protocol 23.1 (variant): What is a challenge for one person is inconsequential for another and vice versa.

Early school days take us out of one world, the family, and drop us into the wider world of experiences with other egos that don't gravitate just around us. We become decidedly less important to other people. We have to learn how to navigate this world of differing styles, opinions, and interests, not to mention the crazy dynamic of who is a friend and who isn't. There were many events that shaped how I would orient in this wider frame of referencing myself and others.

One such event occurred when I was in grade 2 or 3, that is, at six or seven years old. At that time, we had no gym at our school, so the teachers would make us do gymnastics in the school hallway. We would do tumbling on the mats. There was a girl who had white underpants under her black leotard, and every time she tumbled, we could see her underwear. I remember the other boys and myself thinking, feeling really, that the sight was very stimulating, although that word was too mature for our years. Nevertheless, it conveys the interest that was present— somehow, we knew this event held importance, held relevance to us.

We are sexually wired from the womb. But curiously, we boys also knew that this was supposed to be secret. Further, there was an unconscious shift from seeing the girl as a person to seeing her as a girl. Where did that come from? Hormones, sure, but … instinct can be brutal. Impulses drive the human condition so much, they can make it difficult to gain perspective.

Victory Protocol 31: Desire mind is rooted in human biology. Psynaut mind integrates that and goes beyond it.

I was busy learning a lot of things which, after being out there in that empty void of spaciousness before conception, I had no idea were going on in this bardo. And more importantly, I was beginning to discover the difference between outer expression, or appearance, versus what was going on inside. The Japanese have this down pat and even have words for it, *tatemae* and *hon'ne*. Tatemae is how we show up in public, our outer face, and hon'ne are our true feelings and desires that only people very close to us see and maybe not even then.

All societies, not just that of Japan, have a strong conformist side. For example, this was typified by another situation. My grade 2 teacher told my mother at a parent–teacher meeting, "Elbud is such an angel, he doesn't have a mean bone in his body." I wasn't going to argue with this point of view; however, it was the same year when I found myself up against the school wall being attacked by four or five other boys. I have no memory of what the issue was, but I was very clear about my strategy, and that was to knock them all down, which I did. Now, lest you get the idea I was going to grow up to be a Bruce Lee type, I will share with you what most boys know. The advantage was mine as I had nothing to lose, and I could operate solo whereas they had to coordinate their attack. So, I just launched in, and they gave up in no time at all. Was that the same kid who "doesn't have a mean bone in his body?" Perhaps, but it would take a lot of self-reflection to see the harmony between the two.

I hated school. No self-respecting boy should let themselves be tied down to a chair from 9 a.m. to 4 p.m., memorizing stuff that had nothing to do with running around, playing, having big adventures, and otherwise letting one's imagination go wild. Boys probably aren't ready to sit still until, I don't know, fifty! Girls, on the other hand, seem ready for it quite early. School is interesting for them. Okay, generalizations, I know, but …

In grade 2, we had those big fat pencils, and when the teacher decided your printing was clear enough, you could get a fountain pen. Eventually, everybody in the class had a fountain pen except me. Finally, one day the teacher said, "Elbud, I'll just give you the pen, okay?" making it quite clear that although she didn't think my printing was up to snuff, she wasn't going to humiliate me by not letting me have a pen. I didn't know whether to love her or hate her for it, but being eight years old, I didn't dwell on it.

They were going to keep me back in kindergarten because they felt I wasn't ready for grade 1. It seems when all the other kids were having their naps, I insisted on getting everybody up, moving around, and playing. I guess today I'd be diagnosed with ADHD, but luckily in those days, we didn't have any labels, so I was just a brat. My mother called me a "ham," and for the longest time, I thought I was a piece of meat. Later she said I should be an actor, although she wanted me to be a dentist. I didn't understand why—getting me to do anything was like pulling teeth!

Another part of our development as humans is how we handle struggle and thus develop determination. As a re-entering Psynaut, I'd had many such opportunities, but we each have to rebuild those muscles afresh from lifetime to lifetime.

Victory Protocol 3.1 (variant): Karma is forged by the will. The choices we make delineate our path. Our state, therefore, is of our own making, and it can be changed.

One thing school teaches you is how to follow the rules … not that anyone ever thought we did it very well, nor did we think we were learning to follow them. Mostly we thought we were learning to rebel. Yet, it taught us how to stick with something and press through even when we didn't like it. It prepared us for the traditional workforce and relationships with people you're not close to, and how to persevere.

10. Recess

Kids can be cruel, and I was no exception. Sometimes we act like we were cast in *Lord of the Flies*. We used to play shinny, street hockey, and as eight-year-olds would spend more time arguing about the rules than actually playing the game. This is how play is also teaching us how to fit in with others.

By the way, I believe that fundamentalists are like eight-year-olds; they are at the stage of psychic development. They have fixed rules, fixed interpretation, no real negotiation skills, no sense of proportion, or any feeling for a bigger picture. They argue a lot about what's in bounds and out of bounds. Everyone has a tribal, vicious side, and while our religions are meant to tame the savage beast, I think they mostly just bury it. That's not necessarily a bad thing for those people who can't find their way to transforming it.

A case in point: we were playing shinny on a frosty early winter's day when a new boy joined our group. For some undefinable reason, he just didn't fit in. I wonder if this is what early humans felt when they abandoned one of their offspring, when nature's course dictated the parent leave their child to die. Does nature know something we don't? Or is the "nature argument" just rationalization for bad behavior on our part?

That day, a few of the boys started to pick on the new kid by pushing him around. I remember not feeling good about this and so held back, but I could feel the pressure mounting from the rest of my "friends" that I was to join in. Did each of us feel that way? Did the tribal mind overtake the individual sense that this was a mistake? Did all the kids feel they shouldn't be doing this? I don't know. In any case, I joined in the pushing and shoving. Eventually, the new kid left crying, and the rest of us acted like we had just conquered an enemy … "I'm so tough, look at me, don't mess with me" energy. Charming.

The new kid went to Catholic school, so I hadn't seen him around until we accidentally met each other trudging through the snow down the back alley a few days later. He stopped and asked me why I had pushed him around. I had no idea, but feeling pressed by his question, I had to offer an answer that made me sound righteous. Later, of course, I realized that my need to fit in was far more important to me than his feelings of hurt and rejection.

Now I understand war, violence, and the prison-and-hell state of isolation created by our own self-cherishing at the expense of others. But back then, I was just a kid (which admittedly we've used for generations as an excuse for bad behavior). I hope this kid grew up to be a leader of some kind because he showed a wisdom far beyond our years. He looked at me kind of sadly and said, "You can believe whatever you like, but it doesn't make you right." I spent quite a bit of time, for an eight-year-old, telling myself he was a jerk. In spite of my efforts, I never convinced myself, but I managed to keep the demon of shame far from my door, at least for a while. But the conformist stage of ego development can come back to haunt you.

Victory Protocol 20.1 (variant): We train in the six virtues in order to undermine the negative and accentuate the positive, in this case, kind behavior.

Balancing that sad story, there was a boy next door a few years younger than me who was very sick and couldn't leave his house for months. In the cold prairie winter, the days can drag on. So, I'd stand outside in the howling cold and knee-high snow, and entertain Billy through his living room window for hours. Even his parents started to watch me, and word got around the neighborhood. Occasionally I would even attract a small crowd.

But I only had eyes for Billy. I'd fall over, pretending to be a soldier who had gotten shot. I'd fake being chased by monsters, running around and falling in the snow. I'd pretend I was buried and had to struggle to get out (old womb contact there). I'd otherwise act like an idiot, running around in circles, laughing and screaming like a madman. The boy, in his pajamas, would howl and laugh through the window, and since I couldn't hear him, he looked even madder than me. That was a lot of fun for both of us, and sometimes his parents would look at me with an expression I didn't fully understand but which held a hint of a thank-you.

Billy died a few years after that. The grand lesson I took from him is that we're all going to die, and often, we have no idea it is coming. Granted, his death perhaps wasn't a big surprise, but out of everyone I've known who has died, for many, it must have come as quite a shock. Our protective social natures have made humans incredibly successful.

Victory Protocol 32: One of the primary elements of a Psynaut's training is joy. (This is one of seven specified elements.)

While we're out in the snow: it's a funny thing, kids' reactions to temperature. I used to run around without a coat on in -20° F weather. My mother would fret, but I didn't seem to notice the cold. It wasn't unusual for her to send me back outside to look for my coat, having forgotten it on a snowbank or by the curb. Once, I forgot my coat at school and walked home the six or so blocks. When I arrived, my mother asked, "Aren't you freezing?" and I said no. She asked me where my coat was, and I said, "I forgot it at school." To my amazement, she took it in stride this time, and I'm not sure many mothers would these days. And I never caught a cold!

Victory Protocol 9.3, on self-development (Integral): Our self-development as humans tends to follow predictable lines. Step one mixes experiences that develop self-identity with growing cognitive abilities and emerging values as we get older.

These self-development experiences all get mixed in the cauldron of who I am and how I would lead my life. They are also based entirely on tribal precepts that universally enshrine a sense of a fixed, permanent, and independent sense of self.

Some of my strongest memories are of my father; for instance, we used to play catch with a baseball, and on occasion, we'd wrestle (he would win by sitting on me). When he taught me how to ride a two-wheel bicycle, I remember him holding the back of my bike as I teetered down the alley and rushing to pick me up when I fell over. Kids learn quickly—I fell only once while learning, although I fell many times after that.

But my mother is a bit of a blank which is interesting because considering the amount of time I spent with each of them, I was with her much more often. She prepared all the meals, made all the beds, cleaned the whole house, washed all the dishes, washed all our laundry, did the shopping, called us to come in, and told us to get out. She was always there, while Dad was typically at work. Yet, it was as though she were in the background, a supporting character—and Dad was the star. We took my mother for granted, and on this point, she never complained.

It's like how we treat nature: we take clean air and fresh water for granted. Historically, we've assigned them no economic value, and that was also true of mothers at the time. Maybe capitalism is anti-mother in that it values only what it gets, not what it gives. And yet for many of us, mother was the ogre, and father … well, he was all right. So perhaps, the personality of the parent dictates what they do or don't do for you.

It's also very interesting that we typically remember our parents as having failed us, how they treated us unfairly, and how they caused us unresolved pain and misery. We forget that we were probably acting like brats. Sure, there are outright abusive parents, and those children have their work cut out for them, clearing that trauma out of their consciousness. But there are far more cases of us children just being spoiled kids.

Victory Protocol 33: Learning to navigate parents prepares us to navigate school, bosses, and spouses.

Another lesson in ego development had to do with the chasm between the rights of children and the rights of adults. My friend's dad smoked cool cigarettes, and one day, we stole a carton of them, retired to the attic in their garage, and proceeded to gang-smoke a good part of the carton, one right after the other. Curiously, I didn't get sick. But his father showed up and caught us red-handed. He told me that I must tell my parents; he would give me a day to do so, and if I didn't, he would tell them himself. This put me in a panic. But where did I learn to be terrified? How did I know I was in trouble?

That evening, as my parents were getting ready to go out square dancing, I strategized my confession. My mother was typically the last one ready, and I waited until my dad was getting irritated and my mother was rushing to get out the door. As they were headed to the car, I blurted out my transgression. They were so distracted that they barely noticed, and all I remember them saying is, "Uh huh, don't do that again." And they were gone. How I had learned to be so devious, so calculating, I have no idea. But one thing was certain: I was learning how to play the game.

Victory Protocol 9.4 (variant): Our values develop through predictable stages, some of which are: survival, magical thinking, egocentric, absolutist, ambitious, humanistic, global, and unitive.

The two-year-old was now eight, and the ego and its agendas were well in place. The baby just is and does, and we accept that, but once they can walk and talk, the playing field is wider, and the game changes.

Determination is learned, and as long as it isn't squashed, it develops on its own according to a child's natural interest. I didn't have much use for school and the rigor of sitting there paying attention to the teacher drone on, but I did love throwing a football up in the air and then running like mad to catch it. I had a goal: 100 passes and 100 catches without a miss. I'd spend hours and hours doing this during the summer. I'd get to 30 and get overconfident and miss one. Then I'd get to 85 and think, "I got this!" and miss one. The day I reached 97, I said to myself, "Okay, I'll just pretend I caught that one." But I never did get to 100.

11. Church

My parents weren't devoutly religious, although my mother was very spiritual (and psychic, as I have mentioned, but more on that later). My father had a Scottish background and was Presbyterian—very practical, not super imaginative. The Presbyterian Church was about five minutes farther away by car than the United Church. I could get to either one of them on my bike in under ten minutes, but my father decided to switch from Presbyterian to United to save the driving time even though they rarely attended. Very Scottish, very practical, and yes, very Presbyterian.

When I was small, I used to love going to Sunday school because I enjoyed the stories about Jesus. I lobbied to join the adults in the main church once I felt I had outgrown Sunday school. To my chagrin, it was very boring, so I stopped going. In my opinion, the minister had no idea what he was talking about. My mother felt the same, and even though I was only around eight years old, I somehow knew this. Years later, as an adult, and being a minister of sorts myself, I realized his knowledge was intellectual and not experiential.

This seems to be our modern education: that information and knowledge pass for experience and wisdom. Are kids like dogs or cats? Can they sense the difference between somebody who seems nice compared to someone who is actually nice? Can they tell when somebody is pretending to like them but doesn't actually? Or in this case, do kids know when someone appears to speak wisely but hasn't experienced what they are talking about? This is another aspect of the Victory Protocols (typically found in the fine print, which not many read).

Victory Protocol 34: Experience plus compassion equals wisdom. Knowledge plus ambition equals selfishness.

This is about the time I had my first experience with another ethnicity. There were three convenience stores in my neighborhood, all three run by Chinese men. At the time, I didn't take any notice of the fact that they were Chinese; they were just vehicles of delivery for the goodies I was after. One Sunday, I decided I would skip church (notice my parents weren't going either) and instead took my plate offering to one of the Chinese convenience stores, where I bought jawbreakers, played around until church was over, and then went home.

When I arrived, my mother asked me how church was. I replied, "Okay." And then she proceeded to tell me that Mr. Chang had called and said I had spent my church donation on jawbreakers! Caught black-mouthed (since jawbreakers in those days were black). At the time, I thought, "That traitor." But looking back on it, what an incredible thing that he knew my name, knew where I was supposed to be, and took the time and trouble to call my mother to make a better citizen of me. This was even more incredible given that, outside of our convenience store visits, our family didn't know any Chinese people, we didn't associate with any Chinese people, and we didn't socialize with any Chinese people. Yet Mr. Chang made the effort.

Were the situation reversed, I'm almost positive that neither my parents nor any of my friends' parents would even think of doing the same, whether for me or for a child of Chinese parents.

Victory Protocol 35: Western culture breeds a personal ego; Asian culture breeds a collective ego.

Near the end of my father's life, he felt he needed exercise. He thought he was too old for golf, curling, and dancing, so I recommended Tai Chi. He asked me where to take it, and I told him to look in the phone book (he never made it to the internet). So he went downtown for a class held above a Chinese restaurant. I asked him much later how the Tai Chi was going, and he told me he'd stopped. I asked why, and he said, "Because it was taught by an old Chinese guy." What do you do with that? I guess he had forgotten Mr. Chang, but more importantly, he would never have considered himself a racist. They just weren't his people.

The Victory Protocols focus on how our views determine what we see and what we learn. They also show how our views, when left unchallenged, seem perfectly reasonable as long as we surround ourselves with the trappings of our normal, habitual world. So, if you hate racists, you are a racist against racists!

Victory Protocol 36: You are what you hate while you're hating it.

A more familiar protocol says that hate is transformed by mirror-like wisdom. In other words, hate is transformed by understanding the mirror-like reflection of your state of hating.

Victory Protocol 37: We see what we believe.

Did I mention I was a brat? While I was annoying, bent the rules, tried to get whatever I wanted when I wanted it, and was often ill-mannered and badly behaved, nevertheless, from my perspective, I was extremely curious, very interested, and determined to find things out. This is demonstrated by an incident at our local church when I was around eight years old.

It was a father-son evening, and the church had booked a magician for the entertainment. My father and I were in the front row, and every time the magician did a trick, I would jump up on stage to try to figure out how he did it and how it worked. Curiously, my father didn't do much to slow me down. I think the magician did about ten tricks, and I was up there with him every time. At the end of the show, the magician, while probably irritated with me, suggested I learn the trade. On the way home, I got a lecture about respecting people's space, but my father also asked me if I knew how any of the tricks were done. I didn't, but I was determined to find out. The individual was starting to show up, following his own star.

12. Neighbors

One of our neighborhood families was addicted to Coca-Cola. They bought it by the case and drank it almost by the hour. We didn't have that much Coke in our house. (There is some argument about whether the recipe still had cocaine in it back then. Supposedly, cocaine was removed from Coca-Cola in 1929, making you wonder if the stock market crash and the ensuing depression were withdrawal symptoms. The recipe is top secret, so who knows ... although I guess chemists would be able to tell. In any case, that family drank a lot of it.)

One day, when I was about ten, I decided I wanted a Coke, so I entered their house and took one (no one locked their house in those days). I did it again on a few different occasions. They finally realized that someone was consuming their stock, and as I was a frequent visitor in their house, the finger was pointed at me, and justifiably so.

At the time, I had a feeling I wasn't supposed to be stealing sodas, but I did it anyway. Things had changed since helping myself to the neighborhood's milk—I was older, and I was supposed to know better. This was the beginning of learning about ownership, private property, and stealing. I was justifiably scolded, and that behavior ended, at least in terms of neighbors' favorite drinks. The lesson had to be relearned later in terms of public property.

Victory Protocol 38: Most behavior is rooted in habit.

There's habitual behavior, and then there's unmitigated greed. In the old days, Halloween hadn't yet been tainted by razor blades and older kids stealing younger kids' candy. We weren't chaperoned when we went trick-or-treating because it wasn't necessary. We kids had our route planned to cover as much territory as possible in the shortest amount of time, and we took along our pillowcases to gather the goodies. Our strategy was:

- Step 1: Wear a light costume that was easy to move around in.
- Step 2: Hide extra pillowcases in convenient locations to make a switch when one was full. It was best to find a place that was close enough to where we'd expect to fill the first pillowcase so that we didn't have to go very far to pick up the second one.
- Step 3: Be polite and courteous, but don't waste too much time talking to the adults giving out the candy.

This strategy worked for a few years, and as I recall, my maximum loot equalled one and a half pillowcases. It wasn't the record; Tommy always got two full pillowcases, but he was bigger and faster. He ended up in reform school in grade 8. Years later, he was arrested for auto theft, and then he robbed a grocery store and wound up in jail ... so maybe winning the record isn't always the best harbinger of success.

Good parenting is probably more important, at least more than I thought, since his dad was also a thief. We learn from our environment, so it's good to have examples of not only what to be, but also of what not to be. A few years later, this sense of restraint in relationship to authority and the rules kept me just this side of ending up in bigger messes.

We had a neighbor, a widow who lived in a big, old house that was run-down and needed a lot of work. Unlike her neighbors, she had a garden in her front yard instead of a lawn, and an old broken-down fence whereas others had hedges or nice picket fences. We considered her a bit of a witch, and since she didn't have much to do with her neighbors, this idea stuck easily enough. It was also fun to think of her that way. Is this how we learn to scapegoat people, or do we learn that with our siblings? "Who took the cookie? Sister did!"

Victory Protocol 39: Prejudice is rooted in making superficial, categorical differences between groups, and devaluing them in comparison to ourselves and our group.

We were "prejudiced" about non-lawn, old, widowed, eccentric people. Nobody seemed to know much about her, and she kept to herself. I remember when we visited her home the first Halloween in that neighborhood, more as a dare than with any sense of a reward—truly trick-or-treat, but in reverse. When we finally built up the courage to go to her front door, we were surprised at her largesse. She was undoubtedly the poorest neighbor on the block, and she was by far the most generous. We each got an apple, some candy, and some homemade popcorn, which was a first. I learned a very important lesson from her, namely, that the most generous are not always the most personable or the wealthiest. In fact, our wealthiest neighbors were noticeably the stingiest.

Victory Protocol 40: Recognize the wholesome for the wholesome, and support it to recur (this is one of four efforts.)

As we got older, and our interests switched from candy to dollars, our strategy changed. Some older kids told us we could get money by pretending to collect for UNICEF, so we did. People were more generous because they thought we were more selfless for not just seeking candy for ourselves. Is this where the corporate raider gets their start? Did the Enron ethic, or lack thereof, get its start like this? We ran this small-time scam only one year, as our consciences didn't like the feeling. Where did that come from? A large vista had opened on morality and ethics. As my great guru said, "You have to break the rule to understand why it is there. Once you see why it is there, you won't break it, and you won't need to keep it. It will keep itself."

Victory Protocol 41: Once you truly understand for yourself why a certain protocol is there, you won't need to keep it; it will keep itself.

Greed comes in many forms, of course, and the little girl two doors down was another temptation I could not refuse. She was my age, around eight or nine, when we found ourselves in her basement. She took the initiative to remove her pants and underwear, and I was faced with her stark-naked lower half. I was fascinated, stunned, and paralyzed. Her slit was so unique to me as to almost not register—perhaps I was not unlike those Patagonian Indians who couldn't see the European sailing ship until they got on board. She asked if I wasn't going to take my pants down, but since this question didn't seem to register in my consciousness, she decided to do it for me. She reached over and pulled down my pants and underwear, and there we were. She grabbed my penis, and we stood like that for a moment. Girls really do mature earlier.

Victory Protocol 34.1 (variant): Wisdom is the arrival of dead-end speech.

Mothers must have a sixth sense about these things because hers called for us to come upstairs, so we quickly pulled up our pants, but not before I kissed her. This I think was my first real kiss, and I find it indicative of my nature that the nudity came first. Once more, I felt we were "caught" in some terrible transgression, yet innocence and curiosity were all there was in our minds.

Next door to her lived my mentor, guide, and advisor on all things in the thirteen-year-old world: Vernon. He lived in the house where I used to steal Cokes. We would spend a lot of time together, at least when his other friends weren't available. If his friends showed up, it was agreed that either I left or stuck to the background. I didn't mind blending into the scenery, as I was getting a lot more out of it than it was costing me in terms of being ignored.

Victory Protocol 42: We learn almost everything from someone else. For some things though, like wisdom, it requires a very special teacher.

But one of the main things I remember about Vernon was him introducing me to masturbation. He would get an erection, which was no big thing, pun intended, because I could do that too. But he could pump it up and down, and make it eject the white fluid, sperm. This was a new word and experience for me. It was both fascinating and somewhat terrifying; fascinating because I didn't know the penis could do that, and terrifying as he'd get this strange look on his face and make funny sounds.

It left me mostly puzzled because one, I couldn't do it and two, I didn't know why he did. But he sure seemed to enjoy it. One day, Vernon said I should try it, so I did. And while I could get it upright, nothing came out of it, so I gave it up, at least for a few years. I remember the first time I managed to ejaculate, and then I understood why he seemed so happy.

Victory Protocol 43: Some experiences do not arise until the groundwork has been set in place.

But perhaps the most formative experience of those years as Elbud 1.1 was the Christmas before we moved again. I was given a thirty-pound test bow with steel-tipped arrows and a target as a present. I wasn't especially skilled, and it often took two hands for me to pull the arrow out of the target, so you can imagine it had some power.

One summer day, I was outside with a friend. Just for fun, I pulled the bow back to its full draw and shot the arrow straight up in the air. My friend and I promptly forgot about it while we were laughing, and as it came down, it landed right on the crown of my head and bounced off. No blood, no wound, no headache, nothing. We just picked up the arrow and walked away.

Years later, when I practiced kundalini yoga in its Himalayan (Vajrayana) form, known as dumo heat practice, the experience with the arrow returned to me. I felt such a rush, as if an arrow flew from my groin up my spine and into the sky. Exhilarating. And then it was as if the arrow flew back down through the crown of my head and into my groin. At that moment, I again felt the arrow that had hit my head all those many years previously. Who says time is linear?

Victory Protocol 44: Time and space are illusions created by the ego to mark its journey.

Maybe the arrow made things fall apart, but soon after that summer day, my world came tumbling down. It seemed to coincide with our next move, and perhaps puberty had something to do with it, but mostly I think it was because I took risks, pressed for answers, and asked questions that bothered me. I wanted to understand what was happening beyond the platitudes we're served growing up. (The Victory Protocols were developed for just such an inquisitive mind. Most Psynaut applicants have had a difficult time fitting in to the mainstream; it's almost a job requirement.) My sense of self was developing, and my values were starting to emerge without any real intent to form them. Like accretions on a coral reef, the calcification of experience leads to identity.

Victory Protocol 9.5 (variant): Our self-identity develops through predictable stages, some of which are: symbiotic, impulsive, self-protective, conformist, conscientious, and individualistic.

We start as symbiotic organisms, clinging to our mother, developing impulses, desires, and emerging self-protection as our separation becomes more evident. We must conform to survive (see values in VP 35) and try to gain approval until we are wise enough to navigate an individuating path.

I had moved through the first steps, but conforming and individuating were yet to come. My worldview was archaic, ruled by tribal impulse, and I lived in a sense of magic and wonder, untroubled by the mythic struggle I was emersed in. That was about to change drastically.

These stories date from what I called my "daring" phase, aged four to nine, the fearless time, the adventurer spirit, the sense one can do anything. Success is not questioned, and failure is not entertained; one just goes out and does it. It is also a big step in independence as we learn to either move out and away from home or stay closer in and near. I'm not sure if every child feels this way or whether it was particular to my conditioning, but I was a wanderer, a risk taker ... and mouthy. I got those qualities from my mother (For what it's worth, a friend of mine who is an astrologer said it was because I had Mars in Gemini.), or maybe they simply grew out of the Psynaut agenda. I also got some practical, methodical, and conservative elements from my father, or maybe those sprung from my Psynaut development as well. Personally, I don't think it was so much the conditioning although being the youngest, and with five years between each of us siblings, I was in a sense an only child.

My mother was a warrior. She had a deep spirituality and a high contempt for organized religion. She particularly saved her scorn for the ministers whom she felt had no idea what they were talking about. My mother was arrogant at times, fiercely independent, and often questioned authority, which is probably what got in my way as well. Given the times in which she lived, and for a prairie woman, she fit slightly outside the mold, and I guess I followed suit. On the other hand, my father was not a particularly brave man; he was a bureaucrat, but he was steady and reliable. He was also organized, methodical, diligent, and steadfast. Those qualities saved my butt more than once.

Our sense of adventure and our appetite for risk-taking tend to dampen as we get older, so we need to reconnect with these early years in order meet our freedom drives. As youths, we have a daredevil spirit, and the fulfillment of the Protocols requires we reintegrate this energy.

The autonomous individual was emerging more and more every day. He was about to run into other kids who were at the same place in their development. And with this came conflicts. Where do each of us fit in? Seems I wouldn't.

13. Traumas

We moved again, from a tumbling, old, three-story house where the corners of the walls weren't quite square and the floors weren't quite flat to a brand-spanking-new bungalow in the suburbs. Mother was ecstatic, to a large extent because she didn't have to go up and down three floors to clean, make beds, and so on. Perhaps it was an omen of things to come, but I didn't get off to a great start in the new house.

We moved in the summer, and the first thing I missed about the old house was that it had an open veranda on the back end of it which on hot summer nights my brother and I would sleep on. There was a huge oak tree that seemed to embrace that veranda, so while we laid there in bed, we heard the rustling of leaves in the breeze and the moving around of birds and squirrels, our little guardians. Sometimes I would wake up in the night and feel a sense of peace and spacious calm while looking up into the starlit sky. In those days, I didn't think much about the future. I was too busy living in the present, but occasionally, it felt like time and space disappeared and that life and myself were one timeless, spaceless experience that included everything and everybody.

Vastness

Oh, little one
Can you feel me here?
Trembling in the dark
Alone, untethered, adrift
You have no idea
My power is infinite, and I eat little ones first
They're more tender

Run, hide, cower
You laugh from your bed
But I drag you out
Everyone is left behind
You have nowhere to stand
And no one can save you

Untethered could also be a very scary feeling, with no one to catch you. Abandonment was not a happy feeling for a kid, or anyone for that matter. I tried telling this to my brother one night, but he just said, "Don't be an idiot. Shut up and go to sleep. You're keeping me awake." So much for transcendental experiences being universal. But I'm sure he had his at other times, in his own way.

On the second day in the new house, my mother was busy unpacking. She gave me a pack of oil-based crayons to occupy me. We had a big picture window in the front, framing the living room, and behind the living room was an open dining room, so from the front window to the back of the dining room was maybe thirty or forty feet. The east wall was my canvas. I proceeded to draw on this pure, plain, smooth, white wall with my crayons, starting at the living room window and working back towards the dining room from knee height to about shoulder height. While it was not a very big distance on an eight-year-old's scale, unfortunately for my mother, I managed to get halfway down the wall.

When my mother discovered my artistic expression, I was in a state of bliss, absorbed in my creative masterpiece. It came as quite a surprise to me that she was not enamored by my talent. In fact, the screaming and yelling was quite distracting. I thought she was going to kill me, but I got off with a relatively mild slap. It's a good thing parents pull their punches, but also, we kids know we can handle more than they give out. The real trauma of course is not in the slap but in the emotional aggression and rejection. By the time my dad got home from work, things had settled down a bit.

I took advantage of the summer weather to get outside during the day, but pulling up the courage to return home for supper and meet my father's response took a little effort. He was not a very expressive man, but a lot of information and feeling can be expressed in a few words and a look, and he was very clear: the task of rubbing mayonnaise on the wall and then rubbing my masterpiece off with it fell to me.

Victory Protocol 45: The ego takes on an appearance in an attempt to protect from the hurt, and therein lies the trauma.

On the basis that our desire mind is going to be interfered with, we can probably say that every human being is going to be trau-matized not once or twice but a few times (hopefully only a few) throughout our lifetime. I read somewhere that if a person does not see something as traumatic, it isn't. While an experience might not be pleasant or happy, it doesn't necessarily lead to self-destructive guilt, shame, or victimhood.

They say an animal doesn't experience trauma if they escape a deadly attack because they go into a physical shakedown, trembling and shivering, then walk away. Supposedly the trembling and shaking releases the adrenaline or the cortisol that otherwise would get locked into the body and seal the trauma in place. Maybe we need to do the same: shake and quake when things get tough. Then, walk on!

I was born blue, with the umbilical cord strangling me, as you might recall. It produced a fear of being strangled that lasted for decades. At the time, I was coddled and swathed by the hospital staff, and I think that froze the trauma in my body. One day, during a long meditation retreat, that memory resurfaced, and my body went into spasm. I trembled and shook and quaked until my system released the trapped energy. After that, the fear of being strangled evaporated.

It's interesting that I didn't join the Quakers or Shakers who used that kind of catharsis as religious exercise. But we also don't want uncontrolled behavior, either in ourselves or others, so we freeze. Maybe this is why trauma is so difficult to process. Granted, the bigger the shock, the harder to defibrillate, but maybe it's a better solution than twenty years of therapy. I suppose even for low-grade trauma, the same principles apply.

As an older child, I remember having been scolded for some of my schemes, but I just internalized whatever I felt about that. I blocked it out. It would have been better if I had shaken and cried and flailed and then laughed about it and let it go—better too for them, I think.

14. Best Friend

The first real love of my life was a dog. He was a miniature collie, but personally, I always thought he was mostly a wolf. He was an amazing creature; loyal, playful, intelligent, brave, adventuresome … in other words, all those things I'd like to see in myself. Supposedly I won him in a contest, but if truth be told, I think I didn't.

The owners of the local radio station, Rob and Roy, were offering the contest. They also happened to be friends of my parents, so I named the dog Rob Roy, which got shortened to Robbie. I'm sure the owners liked the name but didn't want to be accused of favoritism, so I think they gave the prize dog to some deserving kid, and gave me another pup in the litter and pretended I was the winner.

Youth is filled with strange memories, and one of mine was about said Rob. We used to spend summers at the lake while my dad worked in town and came out on weekends. One weekend, we visited Rob's family on the same lake (which incidentally is where I found out about the dog contest). Rob owned a pistol, and down by the shore he had a target. He would sit on the lawn chair overlooking the lake and fire bullets at it while kids played nearby. As he was telling me about the dog contest, he handed me the revolver, taught me how to aim it, and said, "Go ahead and shoot."

Mind you, I was only eight years old, and I was pretty scared. The only frame of reference I had for guns was hunting. My father, brother, and future brother-in-law would go hunting and come back with ducks and occasionally with deer, so I guess I had already made the connection between guns and death. I summoned up my courage, aimed it at the target, and after what seemed like an interminable amount of time, pulled the trigger. The gun jumped in my hand, and I missed the target of course, but it brought my mother running. She suggested I find other things to do while giving Rob a stern look. I have speculated that this might be why I "won" the contest—Rob was buying my mother off for having contributed to the much-too-early education of her child.

It's amazing to think that humans all live on the same planet but not all in the same world. I recall the world of children only marginally touching that of adults. There was so much going in their world that we had no idea about, like rent and taxes and marriage and divorce, although in those days, divorce was rare. And despite our mothers always insisting they knew exactly what we were up to, the only things they really knew were what they caught us at.

Fundamentally, the world of children isn't all that interesting to adults. But I think adults are making a mistake not to take an interest in it. I remember not really having any problems as a child. Even the problems I had in relationship to my place in the pecking order at school or with friends didn't register as problematic; they were just something I moved through. In this sense, kids are almost awakened but are too dumb to know it. Of course, we never thought we were dumb, which was really the central problem.

Victory Protocol 46: Humans tend to dismiss those who don't serve their needs in some immediate fashion.

Most importantly, I got the dog, and being dismissed didn't really matter. It would have been worse had I been ignored!

I loved that dog. His exploits were legendary, and he has gone down in history as one of the most amazing dogs ever. For instance, our neighbors had a smaller dog, and Robbie used to jump the five-foot fence between our yards, clearing it entirely. The fence also had a bushy hedge in front of it, so making the leap was even more extraordinary. The other dog would grab onto Robbie's tail with its teeth, and Robbie would run around their yard in circles with the other dog hanging onto his tail, all four paws off the ground. They would do this for quite a while until Robbie got tired, and then he would jump back over on our side and rest.

Kids loved Robbie. In the frigid prairie winters, they would all be bundled up in their parkas and scarves and mittens on their way home from school. They would trundle down the alley between two sets of fences of people's backyards. When they got to the top of the alley, maybe six or seven houses away, we could see them from the kitchen window, and we knew Robbie was hiding behind one of the neighbor's fences or our own.

As the kids started coming down the lane, they'd be looking left and right and up and down and in front and behind, wondering where the dog was. And when they were least expecting it, Robbie would leap over the fence, land on top of two or three kids, and spread them like bowling pins. The kids would laugh and giggle and scream, and Robbie would take off over another fence. While they picked themselves up and continued to make their way down the lane, Robbie would secretly run off, either jumping other fences between houses or running out on the street. He would come from another direction and get into another hiding position from where, when they least expected it, he would leap over the fence and do it all over again. This would happen two or three times in a passing, both at lunch and at the end of the day. We laughed so hard that we could barely stand up. It sure helped to pass those long winter days.

Victory Protocol 47: A good heart can sometimes support rough behavior if its motivation is pure.

Robbie didn't like people in uniform (probably an early puppy-hood trauma). He tended to sit on the roof of the car in the driveway, looking out to the street and surveying his domain. The first few times the postman came to deliver the mail, Robbie attacked. Snarling and growling, he backed the postman out onto the street, but he went no farther. One of us would run out and grab Robbie, and as soon as we were there, Robbie had no problem letting the postman walk up to the house. This technique became part of our routine; before he got to our house, one of us would walk down to the street and escort the postman up the sidewalk, all the time petting Robbie as the postman delivered the mail. Eventually, we just took the mail from the postman curbside, and Robbie gave up paying any attention to him whatsoever.

When the police came to arrest my brother for stealing hubcaps a few years later (my brother was five years older), Robbie went into the same hysterics. As far as I know, at least until the lady with the cat, nobody insisted that Robbie be removed. These days, he probably wouldn't last a week before someone complained as we have become so sensitive to danger. (If you're wondering, my brother was let off with a warning.)

In fact, the word "safe" never came up in conversation except for instance, "Is the water safe to drink?" Recently, I was talking to a marketer and made this point about how everyone had to feel safe these days. He was surprised (he was in his forties so was born around 1975 after I had already finished university) that the world had not always been concerned with being safe. I guess the accumulated years and the shift from the 1950s to the 1990s were more traumatic than we thought if "Is it safe?" have become such important words.

Victory Protocol 48: The ego never feels truly safe because it is an illusion (albeit an unconscious one). Ego is a concept held together by other illusory concepts that make it seem real.

I attribute feeling unsafe to a combination of things such as crazy wars, environmental degradation, viruses, limbic capitalism, gratuitously violent movies with ever increasing sociopathic and psychopathic "heroes," and our fascination with dystopian movies. Americans also seem to have an affinity for conspiracy theories probably rooted in violent karma.

Similar to his feelings about the postman and the policeman, Robbie didn't like cats. But unlike the postman and the policeman, Robbie would actually kill cats. He would hunt them like game, and he was consequently banished to my uncle's farm. I understood why, but I was none too pleased to lose my best friend. Robbie was so good at hunting cats that before he became the neighborhood cat assassin, our neighbors insisted we bell him, which we did. But it was futile because Robbie learned to stalk and attack without ringing that bell. We found out that he had killed one of the local cats, panicking a neighboring housewife. Her cat had run through the attached garage, into their house, and into her arms, and Robbie had come tearing after it. He wouldn't have hurt the woman, but imagine a sixty-pound dog coming at you like a freight train.

The fact that he weighed sixty pounds worked for me when I wrestled with him. I'd throw him up in the air, then throw him on the ground and land on him. Then I'd run away, and he'd chase me around the yard, leaping on me from five feet away and laying me flat like an inside linebacker from a football team.

Victory Protocol 49: A Psynaut is called the good friend, a mentor, an experienced and trusted advisor. Trust starts with love.

Years later, by the time Robbie was exiled to the farm, I was old enough to learn how to drive, that is, eleven.

15. Wheels

Robbie was my first big lesson in the views of the world. My relationship with the dog was archaic, even magical, bordering on the mythic. Recognizing, albeit reluctantly, that Robbie was not meant for civilized society and that he had to go to the farm was one of my early steps into the rational world of people having to live together with some common view. In this case, pets needed to act like pets.

A few years later, when my father came in my room and told me that Robbie was missing and presumed dead from eating a poisoned rat, I was strangely unmoved. I wondered about it at the time and felt I was a mean sort of kid, but in retrospect, it's as if that part of my development had come to an end. The pantheistic view had given up its grasp on the past to move into the modern view. However, the amount I've written on Robbie shows us that that primal person is never completely gone!

Victory Protocol 9.6 (variant): Views develop in stages, from archaic to mythic to collective to universalist, with various stages in between.

Years before Robbie died, I began honing my new skills as an automobile driver. My father used to put me in his lap while he was driving through the Parliament building grounds or on quiet country roads and let me steer. I would crank the wheel left and right like I was in a racing car. I learned to make the turns more gradually as I got better and could reach the pedals. My driving was already pretty good when we took Robbie to the farm about six miles south of town.

On the day we had to take Robbie to the farm, I drove him out with Dad by way of the highway, and we dropped him off with my aunt and uncle. It was a sad departure back to town, and the week that followed was rough for me. But when I got home from school Friday afternoon, Robbie had turned up at the house, having run the six miles to our place. We had no idea how he had found his way.

With much pleading, I persuaded my parents to let him stay till Sunday. And on Sunday afternoon, I would drive him, with my dad, back out to the farm. This was my first experience of shared parenting. This would happen every weekend while the weather was good, but when winter came, Robbie stopped coming in. I became a pretty good driver, going out to the farm and back every week.

As winter melted away and spring weather brightened our days, we'd start to predict Robbie's arrival. As soon as the snow had melted enough, Robbie was back in. It was the melting of the snow that told us he was coming into town on the dirt roads not via the highway. How'd he figure that out? How did he know what day Friday was? Because he always showed up on a Friday.

Robbie carried on his murderous ways at the farm chasing rats. And one day, he managed to get what my uncle figured was a poisoned one. They heard him howling in the night and were planning to take him to the vet first thing, but when they got up in the morning, he was nowhere to be found. It's hard for a dog to disappear in the prairies, especially a sick one, but we never did find his body. We even asked the highway crews to keep an eye out for him when they cut the grass on the side of the road near my uncle's farm, but no sign. Robbie disappeared into thin air, probably hanging out somewhere in the Alaya (see VP 4 and 4.1).

On the subject of driving, I should tell you about the time I got a warning from a pleasant RCMP cop for speeding. My dad had an agricultural administrative job that in the summers took him around the state to visit various regional offices and also some local farmers, getting a feel for the land. As a kid, I would sometimes accompany him for fun during the summer holidays.

Arrogance is such a strange thing. For no good reason, I would walk around these little farm towns as the big city kid, like I was a movie star or something. The local kids were not impressed.

Victory Protocol 50: Superior feelings, inferiority complex. Inferior feelings, superiority complex.

There was one town, I think it was called Tisdale, that had about five thousand people and maybe ten or fifteen streets. We always got a big kick out of the house numbers, like 2568 Elm Street. Where were they starting their numbering from? Toronto?

On the way back from one of these jaunts, my father was tired, so I drove. If you know small prairie towns, you know some of them aren't even towns, and as I was zipping through a place with two grain elevators, a garage, and a little restaurant at about eighty miles an hour, the cops pulled me over. My dad was sound asleep, and he only woke up when I rolled down my window and the cop started talking.

"How old are you, son?" he asked.

"Sixteen," I lied.

"Can I see your driver's license?"

"I forgot it at home."

"Sir," he addressed my father, "how old is your son?"

"Twelve," my dad replied.

"Okay, and how fast do you think you were going?" he asked.

"About seventy," I lied. (The speed limit was sixty-five then.)

"Uh huh ... you were doing about eighty. Okay, sir, take over from your son and don't let him drive again on the highway until he has a license." And off we went.

In those days, every prairie kid learned to drive young, typically on farm machinery, so it wasn't unusual to see a kid who could barely reach the pedals driving something or other.

16. School Daze

Do we ever really know ourselves?

Childhood is fraught with these kinds of dilemmas. Who am I? Who do you think I am? And for most kids, while it is an exhilarating part of life, it's also often a painful time. We learn how to fit in as we try to be liked and approved of. I was no exception. It was a new neighborhood and a new school.

School is where it all went to shit for my ego and was probably the beginning of my re-awakening. I never quite fit in after the new move, probably because I was just too much. And also, perhaps too sensitive. It was about this time that my mother said, "Elbud, you're too sensitive," and I replied, "Maybe, but Mom, you're not sensitive enough." Regardless, my sensitivity didn't help with my school career. Not only was I uninterested in school, I also didn't have many social skills.

The proof came on the second day in my new school when I got into a fight with a boy named Alex. I can't remember what started the fight or why, but we were in the playground, and he punched me. It didn't really hurt, but I was so shocked that I didn't respond. I was more upset that he wanted to hit me. This was not the old Elbud; this was a new creature, more sensitive, less confident, and seemingly getting a lot of unwanted attention because I wasn't very popular. Maybe every twelve-year-old feels this way, but it would be many years before I felt back on my game.

Alex also brought home some very interesting lessons about karma (VP 3, 3.1). Karma basically means the law of cause and effect, or action and reaction; "So you sow, so shall ye reap" in Christian terms.

After Alex hit me, we became friends at a distance. On a few occasions, while we were playing in his house, his mother, tired of us, would say, "Why don't you boys go play in the traffic!" I found this a very odd thing to say. But it became almost prescient years later when as a young teenager and a relatively new driver, Alex was driving his drunk friends home from the lake. They got into an accident, and everyone in the other car was killed. Alex and friends survived. He had the presence of mind, when the cops showed up, to ask for a breathalyzer to prove he had not been drinking. Alex was always overconfident in his opinion of himself which I could relate to until I arrived in that new school and neighborhood. However, the accident changed him. It was some years later when I saw him again at the university. I asked him how he was doing and what he was studying. He was going to become a church minister.

Victory Protocol 9.7 (variant): The ego needs to be constantly reassured/affirmed for mental and emotional stability.

Later, after the Psynaut triggers got pressed, and I pursued a spiritual path myself, I couldn't help thinking that this story winds up in itself somehow. Did his hitting me pry open a secret hallway?

Another karmic rebound came up around my being mean. Remember that boy who asked me why I picked on him? Well, payback finally arrived. One Saturday in grade 7, when I was about twelve years old, a bunch of us boys went to a Saturday matinee. I went out to go to the bathroom, and when I came back, everybody except one boy had moved five or six rows over in an almost empty theater. I felt devastated, and in an attempt to buy Tom's loyalty, I offered to get him some popcorn. I went out to get the popcorn, and when I returned, he too had joined the other boys, leaving me by myself. I was persona non grata, and my self-confidence rapidly eroded.

When the movie was over, we all ended up on the street, and since we lived in the same neighborhood, we were going the same direction. One or two of them told me in no uncertain terms that I was not welcome, and the rest went along at best, or agreed at worst. It was a very long walk. But it taught me a very important lesson.

Popular and unpopular are very fickle positions. Since I had been so popular before, or so I thought, and was so unpopular now, I was coming to understand that there was no real refuge in friends. Friendship is based on common views and shared experiences, so if either of these changes too much, the friendship tends to evaporate or dissolve. Friends come and go, marriages come and go, and in the end, you're left with yourself.

How you live with yourself, the state you're in, what your work is, and what you bring to the social table determine your reality. And while I got more skillful over the years with negotiating social, gender, and coworker relations and regained some popularity in the process, I would never again trust relationships built on personality.

Victory Protocol 9.8: Social skills can be learned. But true social skills require seeing through the illusion of a fixed sense of self.

Karma is inexorable, and this is one of the main points of the Victory Protocols. We each build our own karma, and so do our communities, nations, and species.

In future years, after I had done much work therapeutically and meditatively, I realized the only refuge was the clear, spacious mind, radiant and blissful, and the only work to do was compassion. Everyone struggles and suffers, but careers, friendships, and spouses won't resolve them. So, the *karma yoga*, how we manifest in the world, is how we demonstrate compassion for all those beings, including ourselves, who might feel lonely and unloved, rejected or abandoned. There is no teacher like suffering (VP 8), except perhaps impermanence—and in the end, they are probably the same thing.

It becomes more difficult when people think they're happy. They don't realize that everyone lives through two, three, or four traumas. And typically, when old age shows up, very few people are going to have much interest in what your life was like except insofar as you have served others with compassion and kindness.

This is what I learned in those years. The boys weren't inherently mean or cruel; they were just acting out *Lord of the Flies* as instinctual creatures looking for their best advantage. I was their Jew, their nigger, their Indian, their woman, their queer. I was somebody to rally against to help them define what they were for.

But let's be clear: some children never recover from these kinds of trauma and can sometimes end up as criminals, addicts, or misfits, and they can even commit suicide.

Victory Protocol 51: It is often from the "rejected" class that many Psynauts get their start.

I wasn't any more popular with the girls either. After Judo practice one Saturday afternoon, I crashed a party, which was my first mistake. They were playing a game where you get under a blanket and are asked to remove your clothes one item at a time. The point of the game is that when you say to remove the blanket, the game is over. I didn't know that at the time. Two or three other kids had gone first and took off their sweater or their pants, leaving themselves in their underwear, and then just got up from under the blanket. I thought this was pretty silly. When it was my turn, I had just returned from the gym at the YMCA and had thrown my clothes over my sweats, and my underwear was in my pocket. So, as I removed each piece of clothing, I eventually got down to my sweats, which no one knew I had on, and as a last offering, I threw out my underwear. I then jumped up from under the blanket, thinking I had been quite clever. But all the kids, especially the girls, thought I was just a jerk and were shocked that I would get naked even though I still had my sweats on. Go figure—when you're popular, you can do anything, and when you're not, you can't do anything.

This was proven to me very clearly a few days later. I was not the least popular kid in my grade; that title was reserved for a very big, overweight kid, Thomas, with worse social skills than me. Both of us being at the bottom end of popularity rankings, we were friendly with each other, and one day, I asked him, "Why are you so fat?" He replied that he had a thyroid problem, that he didn't actually eat much, and that he was on medication. He said no one ever believed him when he told them. We were friends after that, and I stood up for him as best I could, although not very successfully given my own lowly status.

One day, we were in a social situation, and he came in and said, "Wow, did you see the Roughriders win the football game?" Everybody just groaned and raised their eyes as if to say, "What a jerk." Two seconds later, Gordon, the most popular kid in the class, came in and said, "Wow, did you see the Roughriders win the football game?" And everybody cooed with amazement at Gordon's wit, charm, and brilliance.

This was another big lesson for me, that popularity and success aren't necessarily deserved (nor are lack of popularity and failure). I made a big mistake of pointing this out to the other kids at the time, and I was promptly relegated back to the Thomas enclave. Thomas was fat and awkward, and I was too brash and challenging.

Victory Protocol 52: Social intelligence usually means you fit nicely in the middle of the paradigm of your culture.

Gordon, for one, deserved his popularity. He was always nice to me, he always treated me as a friend, and he never rejected or excluded me. I learned a big lesson from him that was long overdue. A human of true worth treats everyone with respect and kindness, even if they don't particularly like them or agree with them. This also is a form of karma. And while every individual has his or her karma, so does every nation.

The powerful nations, like powerful people, tend to be arrogant and self-important. It is only a matter of time before that attitude comes back to haunt them. Hubris too has payback. Take for example Sam Walton, the founder of Walmart. While his kids didn't want anything to do with him and were arguing over the money, he supposedly said on his deathbed that he had blown his life. He wasn't referring to his great financial success but rather to his failure as a person in regard to his family and friends.

But school days weren't all misery. A great confidence-building experience occurred when we were playing football in grade 7 (at twelve years old). Actually, we called it "schmear," and the rules were simple: whoever had the ball you schmeared. In other words, you tried to lie them flat with as much force as you could muster. No one ever seemed to get very hurt; I suppose it was more like rugby than American football. We added a Jewish sch to smear to give a sonic emphasis to the complete devastation of your opponent.

During one particular game, the biggest kid in the school, who was almost twice everyone else's size and one grade ahead of me, was running full tilt with the ball. Typically, we just got out of his way as he tended to bowl everyone over. Without thinking, I bent over at the waist and turned sideways, as though I was going be turned into a bowling pin and put into orbit. When he ran into me, he went flying, did a complete somersault in the air, and landed on his face. My center of gravity was below his own. I was as surprised as anyone, but my social stock certainly went up, not only for laying him flat but also for standing in for the charge. He had a mean temper sometimes, and after he got up, he tried to pick a fight with me, but everybody was laughing so hard that he gave it up as a lost cause.

Victory Protocol 53: Sometimes a small shift in behavior can have significant, unforeseen consequences.

It is often the less popular youths that become the more interesting adults. This is probably because they have to reach beyond the status quo to find a place they can thrive. This drives exploration, discovery, and challenges that tend to make you a more dynamic individual.

Our paths can emerge from the smallest things, and life experiences come to not only build and shape our faith but also to challenge and test it. In fact, faith is a kind of roadmap to our identity; it molds how we meet the world and determines who we become.

Victory Protocol 54: Your faith shall set you free.

Faith doesn't necessarily mean a belief in something. It can also mean a trust that if we reach out to find a better alternative, we'll find it. It is almost a tautology that the status quo is faithless since it keeps everyone in the same prison of normalcy.

One more traditional test of faith occurred when I was in grade 6. I was not the best in the class; in fact, I was close to the worst. I barely passed all throughout grade school. We had a math test coming up, and I felt out of my depth. The morning of the test, I prayed to God, "God, if you give me a good grade, I'll believe in you forever and be a good person." When I got to class, I sat down calm as an ice cube in the

Arctic and took the test. I finished in five minutes, and as I handed it in, the teacher was very surprised, as I was typically one of the last to finish. She encouraged me to check it over, knowing my history. But, supremely confident, I said no, it was good, and returned to my desk. She checked it, and I had gotten all the questions right, 100%. She went very quiet, walked down to my seat, and looked for how I had cheated.

She even took me to the principal, who asked me if I had cheated. I said, "No, God took the test for me." You would think this would make me a religious fanatic, and maybe later it did, but I proceeded to forget about what I had promised God. I do think my trust, ease, and calm helped me pull out the knowledge I had been taught in school, and my lack of tension allowed that knowledge to flow through. Nevertheless, my attitude in denying the process put the ego back on top, and the karma ripened after that: I returned to being a terrible student.

I would remember this in later years when I was a teacher and saw the karmic down-flow of lack of *parami, or "virtue."* Paramis highlight that pride, self-centeredness, overindulgence, prudery, and so on are *not* virtues.

I was getting to that age when the politics of egos were emerging into what would become my persona but without any sense of it happening to me. This persona was going to make itself known via, in part, my three lower chakras. The three lower chakras are about resources (money), sex (identity), and independence (control).

Victory Protocol 55: The shadow aspects of our psyches revolve around the lower three chakras.

My struggles started formulating around me as the individual emerged from the child. Usually, the midlife crisis is what shows you the paradox contained in, and possible transcendence of, inherited belief patterns and their symbols. For me, such a crisis started in grade school and lasted into my twenties. In other words, my faith in "the system" was dissolving as fast as it was supposed to be building. It showed up as incidents involving these very chakras.

The shadow can have huge power.

These last years of public school (until grade 8) are filled with experiences that at the time we take for granted but which later have a large impact on our lives. For instance, we had new next-door neighbors. They seemed pretty cool, but appearances can be deceiving. They had a son, Doug, about my age but who was from my perspective a bit of a nerd. So, we didn't have much to do with each other.

One summer day, I was headed out to play football with some friends, and my mother suggested I take Doug with me. I did not think this was a good idea, as I thought Doug would be a bust, but she insisted. As I was leaving the house, Doug happened to be standing there. In a surge of generosity, and in spite of myself, I asked him if he wanted to come play football. He said yes. I suggested he change his clothes. He was always very immaculately dressed for a kid, and he was going to get very dirty. But he said he was good, these were his "rough" clothes, so I said let's go then. But as we were walking away from the house, his mother called out and asked him where he was going. He told her he was going to play football with me.

She said he couldn't go out looking like that, and he needed to come in and change his clothes. But when he came out after changing, Doug was even more dressed up. It was ridiculous that the woman had no idea what a boy was, at least in those terms. Anyway, we went to play football. We had a great time, he got filthy, his clothes got torn, he got a bloody nose … and he was just fine.

When we returned home, his mother happened to be at the front door. She freaked and told Doug to get in the house immediately. I sure felt sorry for him. Years later, after I had moved away to go to university, I heard from my mother that Doug had jumped off the 15th floor of a local hotel.

There is a saying that the road to hell is paved with good intentions. I'm sure Doug's mother had her son's best interests at heart, but this story taught me another lesson: we can have the very best of intentions and views (from her perspective), but they can be destructive (from someone else's perspective, namely, Doug's). Doug had told me he was going to enroll in a university far from our hometown, but his mother had forbidden it, insisting that he live at home until he was married and that she would have to approve anyone he chose to marry. The day I heard this from Doug, before I went away, I remember thinking, "This isn't going to end well."

Many years later, when I was in class, my teacher started a quote and couldn't remember the end, so I filled it in for him. In some ways, it has been my motto throughout life. It is from "Invictus," a poem written by William Ernest Henley in 1875:

> *It matters not how strait the gate,*
> *How charged with punishments the scroll.*
> *I am the master of my fate;*
> *I am the captain of my soul.*

17. Only the Shadow Knows

The power of the shadow has been called a moral issue. It is also an unconscious player in our psyches and takes considerable effort to raise from the depths to the light of day. "Why bother?" we might ask, "Can't we just leave it alone?" Unfortunately, most if not all of life's misery and pain is rooted in the shadow's embrace. And most of our actions that cause harm and hurt stem from its blind force.

So, what was this shadow about to wreak havoc on my life? According to my friend Carl Jung, the shadow consists of the personality "drives" that are considered unacceptable by our egos and, by extension, society. These drives get projected out into the world and often onto others. The shadow almost always has a sexual element, as we shall see shortly, but debauched, aggressive, or suicidal elements can also be present. Even the passive and meek can have suppressed shadow forces. Our sense of the devil ("lived" spelled backwards, so that which is not lived) lies in the repressed shadow.

The shadow lives in our lower three chakras, which are concerned with survival, identity, and control. These revolve around resources (money), self-expression (sex), and independence (being in control). Everyone has a shadow, and each of us must walk alone to meet it. Once its destructive force is liberated (by seeing it as the potential for much greater energy in the form of kindness and compassion), the shadow becomes a force for love.

Victory Protocol 56: There are many chakras in the body with different ways to count them. Here we talk of seven. The lower three are roughly at the perineum, the sacral area (lower spine), and solar plexus (abdomen).

The emerging Psynaut faces a chicken-or-the-egg argument: does the shadow sprout the Psynaut, or does the Psynaut plunge the shadow?

No one wants to meet their shadow. When I did, I discovered I wasn't as wonderful as I thought I was. Dark forces hide in conventional living, but while these appear as demons to the ego, they are also messengers of truth and freedom when understood.

Destruction

Clever words, smart ideas, funny theories
Do you think these will protect you?
You hide in plain sight, and I see all
You think it's all about your "me"
Well, let me introduce my selves

I am
Abraxas, Amon, Behemoth, Bhairava, Beelzebub, Bael,

I am
Chiang-shih, Garuda, Hecate, Hel, Incubus, Jinn,

I am
Lucifer, Mephistopheles, Moloch, Mamman, Pretas,

I am
Seraphim, Satan, Succubus, Tezcatlipoca,
Torngarsuk, Vampire, Zagan

I am
Many more

Your puny name and silly world
I put in my coffins
I tear off the flesh and powder your bones
Worse, I make you first ignored and then forgotten

On a few occasions, I sat with my parents as they watched some program that occasionally involved kissing. In those days, it was all very tame, and you'd see the stars held in a lip-locked embrace, but there was none of that open-mouth, tongues-rolling-around business, which came later. With this imagery in my mind, I would bike over to the old neighborhood and meet a girl who had lived down the street from me. We would talk and play, and one day, I asked her if she had seen the TV show with the man and woman kissing. She looked at me kind of funny and said yes, and as I stood there figuring out my next move, she asked me if I would like to try it with her. (I'm not claiming innocence by any means, but I just want you to know that three times now the girl had been the initiator.)

We proceeded to take each other in our arms like in the movies and pressed our lips together, moving our heads around and kind of wiggling. We did this for what seemed like hours, just rolling around, lip to lip, and moving our heads back and forth until we got tired and went back to playing. She wanted to play house, and I wanted to go on adventures—some things just don't change.

Sexuality doesn't arise as some nice talent, like learning to read and write. It's a force; it runs you like wolves chasing deer. Mostly, one doesn't think of controlling it; one wonders what to do with it!

Our family sometimes spent summers at the lake. It was a great joy, as it felt like another planet, although it was only twenty miles from town. We would swim, run around, and cavort. We were just about at the age when fascination with girls was overtaking other interests. There was one event I was sorry to have missed for many years afterwards.

Our cottage had walls that didn't go right to the ceiling. We boys would change in one room, and the girls would change in another. Because I had an older sister, she also had older friends. I was about nine, so she would have been nineteen. One day, when the girls were in their room changing into their bathing suits, my friend and I peeked over the divider. Did they know we were there? I certainly thought we were making enough noise, but then so were they. In any case, just as it came to the great moment where all would be revealed, my mother called me from the other room, and I had to leave. By the time I got back, the girls had changed and gone out while my friend just stood there, dumbstruck and speechless. I had missed the entire event.

On this note, what is the fascination with the naked female body? I was told women aren't nearly as interested in seeing naked men. They say men tend to be object-oriented and women more relationally focused. I suspect it also has to do with giving birth and breastfeeding. Boys aren't mother, she is unreachable; girls can be more accessible.. From my perspective, it also has to do with how women carry themselves and the likelihood that if something were to happen between a man and a woman, it would be initiated by the woman with some sort of invitation, if only a look. This has been true in my experience—on those occasions when I have initiated without that look, it hasn't gone very well or very far.

However, it's not all sweet and innocent, as the old movies would have had us believe. After I decided it wasn't really crazy but that the world was only partially nuts (or, as the Buddha said, filled with people who are like "unbaked bread"), I also had to come to terms with drives and instincts that can override and demolish our culture's professed values and beliefs. And while I'm not proud of this next story, I think it's important to record for us to understand what goes on in the minds of children before they have been fully programmed to do the "right thing." Like William Golding's *Lord of the Flies*, we can be savages.

What I call The Lord of the Flies Incident was not cute. My friends and I would run down the railroad tracks, and it took a week or two of summer to get our feet hard enough to be comfortable speeding down the sides of the rails on the crushed gravel. One particular day, as I was running down the tracks after returning from the beach, there was a pretty girl walking the other way. Her bathing suit had ridden up a bit, and I could see her bum. The desire to have sex with her was overpowering, and I found myself following her. I was about eleven or twelve, and pubescence was just around the corner. My imagination went to pulling her into the bushes and having sex, whatever that was (since I didn't actually know yet), by the railroad tracks. At the same time, I was terrified she'd say no or get me into trouble somehow, so I planned to jump her from behind so she couldn't see me and have my way with her.

Then naturally I'd have to kill her because if she saw me, I'd be in for it. I followed her for about five minutes, figuring out a strategy without any sense of her being a person—she was just an object in my scope. Luckily, the five minutes was enough time to get a grip, and I gave it up, turned around, and went home. I don't think she had even noticed me. I expect the fear of consequences had brought me to my senses, but there was a lingering feeling that the desire was much bigger than me …

Appetite

I am appetite
I take what I want
Don't get in my way
Others don't exist for me
Everything is mine
Don't get in my way
I'll destroy you
Fool, you won't see me coming

I tell you it's all yours for the taking
I am always raising the bar and
Making it more and more and more
But you never get there
You're always searching, grasping, reaching
You can't have it, or you get it and it's taken away

I am the voice that says,
Give me, mine, get out of my way
I am Golem
And you think you deserve it
Ha, ha, ha, see the corpses?

Victory Protocol 57: In Buddhism, moral dread and shame are considered wholesome.

Where do we learn that other people are to be treated as we treat ourselves? I was taught the Golden Rule, but it doesn't mean anything until you've suffered and been on the receiving end. I still didn't get it, and I expect because the sexual drive isn't bad, it's good. But we are taught to meet it is as if it is somehow bad unless it conforms to society's standards, and frankly, the sex drive doesn't care about society. I expect the reason we treat it badly is not from the act but because the sex drive doesn't care about "law and order." That of course doesn't mean it has to be lawless either. Thus, shadow work!

I tell this story because I don't believe I was unusual. I think lots of young boys and girls, new to their sexuality, repressed by their society and its handling of the subject, must work it out on their own. And not every boy or girl succeeds, unfortunately. If ever there were a case for sex education, surely mine was an example. Nothing happened in my case, but far too often, others take action with destructive consequences. But what's important to know is that it seems to be a universal impulse, at least in boys, to "go and get it." We never had sex education in my day, and I don't know how it has changed. But because of that feeling, and given that rape and assault cases are proliferating, something is not working. What the adults are missing is that kids don't care what adults think but are not aware enough to see the results of the education, or lack thereof, that is being pressed upon them.

Those years from ages ten to twelve were challenging and exciting. Budding sexuality, along with where you fit in the social matrix, are major themes. As groups of boys, we would find some excuse to take our clothes off, run around naked, and generally challenge each other for penis-based entertainment. For instance, one evening over at Gordon's house while his parents were out, we dreamed up strange challenges for each other like running naked down the street ringing doorbells or grabbing each other's penis, playing with our own, or dancing in the window naked.

There was a lot of talk of the girls that were developing breasts and what we'd like to do with them, but at a fundamental level, we had no idea what we were talking about. It's not that we weren't sexually "mature," but we weren't yet ready to do anything about it beyond posturing. When we met these girls at school, we were tongue-tied even as we ogled. That was all going to change very quickly in the next year or two. By the end of grade 8, at about thirteen years old, our attention had shifted from each other onto girls almost exclusively. There may have been boys who preferred to focus on other boys, but in those days, no one admitted it.

I was sent to the principal's office for acting up one day (I was bored silly in school). I met a girl from the other grade 8 class who was sent there for the same reason. She had developed early, and her breasts stimulated a lot of talk amongst the boys. We were waiting in his office, just her and me sitting there. I took my first risky venture into something I was now capable of following through on as pubescence had arrived: I told her she had nice titties and how I'd like to feel them. To my surprise and shock, she said, "Okay, then go ahead," and that stopped me cold. She laughed, and just then, the principal arrived to save me from paralysis if not embarrassment.

My faith in my own "mastery" was weakened that day. But I learned my sexual interest had repercussions when projected out into the world, and it would not always be welcome. I don't think my embarrassment was so much because I wouldn't or didn't want to touch her but because her attitude was not one of interest but of rejection. She was putting me down by calling my number on what I didn't realize at the time was rude behavior.

Around that time, I still had a babysitter. I really didn't need one, but my parents were uncomfortable leaving me alone, so they asked the girl next door, a beautiful redhead named Marion, to "kind of watch me." I don't know just when I started to see girls as pretty, but she was. Marion was only two grades ahead and had already emerged into her woman's body, albeit not by much. We were watching TV together on the couch, and I was doing everything I could to kiss her, fondle her, and get her clothes off. While she seemed to be enjoying the attention, she didn't want to go there; she told me about periods. I heard what she said but didn't really get the concept. Still, we had a pleasant kind of battle/dance. She was getting some touch that she could control, and I was discovering girls in a new way.

Marion actually had a crush on my older brother which I absolutely couldn't understand. Our occasional "relationship" went on for about a year, with me trying to get her to go further and her keeping me from going too far. In a masochistic sort of way, it was very pleasant since we both were enjoying something about it while also being slightly frustrated.

On another occasion, there was the girl who lived near us with whom I made out and fondled. While I tried to get her to have sex, we never quite got that far. And then there was the girl who disappeared in grade 8 (around thirteen years old). She had become pregnant and was removed from school. We never saw her again. It was like she had the plague or something—the deafening volume of silence around the whole issue from everyone showed how repressed, suppressed, and depressed our society was for lack of a sexual education. It was 1962.

Our Western culture has been notoriously uptight about sexuality (and female sexuality in particular), and when we exported our culture to the new world, too often leaders in those communities were repressed, suppressed, and depressed. And while most of the various churches preach chastity and restraint, their emissaries may be guilty of succumbing to desire themselves.

Surely, we need a new look at the reality of young people's sexual drives and how to put them to enjoyable and healthy exploration. Perhaps this would eliminate inappropriate behavior that seems to proliferate in a culture that sells sex to children and adults alike while at the same time promoting a view that sex is bad. We see this in teenage horror movies, wherein the sin (all horror movies focus around sin) is typically about sex or the sexual drive—the young couple who has easy sex always die first.

But I suspect this kind of dialogue doesn't appear in the classroom or from parents or teachers. I suspect further that any kind of shadow material is taboo since it has been for centuries. But what we don't realize is that not addressing it means that its very existence is denied and also that there will be unfortunate individuals on both sides of the victim/victimizer fence that are going to suffer for it.

The Victory Protocols address the shadow material around sex and other shadow issues, but the trickiest part of the protocols is and has been around sex in particular. The upshot is that while we have some good social reasons for monogamy, chiefly around child-rearing and property values, there has never been a truly monogamous culture. With the advent of birth control and feminism—in the sense that women are in control of their own bodies and their own decisions economically and biologically—we have entered a new paradigm. Add to that the fact that the number-one form of household in the United States is single people living alone, we can see that marriage and the nuclear family are in decline.

This trend contributes to the loosening of libido that otherwise would have been suppressed by society. We see that in television shows that are only now one step away from pornography. Not so long ago, naked breasts on TV must have been "expensive" to show as their appearance was rare. But they must have become very "cheap" because now they're everywhere. The only visual missing in TV series now is an actual shot of an exposed vagina and a penis entering it … and shows are getting close. When does it become pornography? Is it when a human in the experience has been reduced to only a body? One of the lesser-known Victory Protocols has to do with this subject under the title of karmamudra:

Victory Protocol 58: Using sexual intercourse can foster an awakening experience if engaged in with shadow elements in the light.

I think my experiences were formative in what later became my theory about gender relations. Leaving aside for the moment the LGBTQ+

identities and just talking about the majority, male and female, it seems to me that healthy and probably successful gender dialogue is based on a few things. First is the "look" and expression of interest; next, the "invite" typically coming from the female ("Interested? Not interested?"). If this is reciprocal, there can be an "approach" followed by an "invite" or request for further engagement. "Holding one's gaze" can invite further engagement (or not) by smiling. At any point in the process, either one or both can step back or call it off, and they can depart as friends, or they can pursue a gradually deepening relationship. In our modern world, I'm not sure this process has changed much since women in general are still very clear about not looking in order to avoid an offer. And while not every look implies an invitation, it seems there is no invitation without the look.

18. More Shadows

Not all desire-based shadow material comes from sexual exploits. Boundary lessons come in many forms, such as drinking, stealing, killing, vilifying, and extreme sports. Typically, shadow material includes hidden issues around money and control as well.

Kids can be so dumb! One evening, I drank almost an entire bottle of my parents' wine. To hide my transgression, I filled the bottle with water. (If they ever noticed, they never said anything to me, probably blaming my older brother who would've denied it.) I then got on my bicycle and rode over to the schoolyard, falling off repeatedly along the way. When I got there, I met a school friend, and he asked what was wrong with me. I told him I had drank a whole bottle of wine which he did not believe.

Why do we do these things? Other than adolescent idiocy, I think it helps build confidence. You might ask how drinking an entire bottle of wine built my confidence, and I'm not sure of the answer, except perhaps that the altered state of drunkenness and my ability to navigate it produced a surety that I could handle myself under altered conditions. Remember as a kid spinning around in a circle until you fell over and fainted for a moment? The altered state of consciousness that most kids seem to live in gradually dissolves with age as the "real"-world concerns of work and relationships take over.

I could also add that holding my wine was going to be helpful later in life when I ran into marijuana, LSD, and other mind-altering substances often taken under bizarre conditions, in foreign countries, and with unfamiliar companions. Not a great recipe for success, but again, confidence-building in that I managed to get through it all.

I don't know whether this risky behavior instilled in me an amoral attitude, but in another situation not long after, Gordon and I found ourselves in a Zellers store with another friend. We were looking at the sunglasses and decided to steal them. We got out of the store without incident and went home. I tried to keep the sunglasses away from my mother's attention, but she saw them and asked me where I had gotten them. I lied and said I had found them. She revealed that the mother of the third friend had called; her son had confessed that we'd all stolen a pair. My mother said I needed to take them back to the store, tell the manager I had stolen them, and apologize. I did take them back to the store and put them back on the rack, but I never confessed the crime to the manager, figuring that since the sunglasses had been returned, no crime had been committed.

As kids, we'd dress up in dark clothes on summer nights and raid our neighbor's gardens by jumping over fences, crawling on the ground like attacking soldiers, and destroying the enemy by munching carrots, devouring peas and beans, and gobbling rhubarb. We'd even bring our own sugar and salt for the radishes! Of course, when Mom served these at home, we'd turn up our noses. We didn't really see it as stealing—more like resource redistribution.

Then there are the physical things kids put themselves through. For instance, in those days there were a lot of outdoor skating rinks, and we used them in all sorts of weather. The girls would tend to do figure skating, and the boys would play hockey. Our hockey games often took place in the evening when temperatures could plummet to -30 degrees Fahrenheit. Playing outside with a pair of skates on and one heavy pair of socks did not prevent your feet from freezing. By the time the first period was over, everyone's feet were numb.

There was a wood shack with a big coal heater run by a Parks employee, and we all gathered around the heater to warm ourselves up between periods, but frozen feet don't like the heat, and they hurt like hell. It was the old Parks guy who said, "You want to take off your socks, go out in the snow, and walk around." As counterintuitive as it sounds, it worked. By the end of the rest break, you were ready to get out, play the second period, and freeze your feet again.

Years and years later, when my meditation teacher had us engaged in an exercise from the Western mysteries that involved running around the Temple in our bare feet in the snow, a few people got upset that their feet had almost frozen. I gave them the advice of that old Parks man, and they were very thankful that it worked in spite of their reasonable impression that it was crazy.

I have no shortage of examples of the kinds of things we'd get up to as kids. There was the time I was playing football and got clothes-hung which put my spine out—a pinched nerve. That required chiropractic treatment. That injury stayed with me into my thirties and finally dissolved in a meditation retreat.

Occasionally, we'd play on construction sites. In one instance, there were two five-story apartment buildings going up side by side. We laid two wooden planks over the short distance between them on the top floor, and walked across. Not smart, but no one died.

We rode our bikes dangerously over hill and dale, reckless and without restraint. No one I knew ever got seriously hurt. The word "safety" was not part of our vernacular, and fear was never mentioned. True, some kids somewhere probably died. Was this the price of living free? Nowadays safety rules everything, and most kids are on a regime of drugs that keep nurses at summer camps fully employed to dispense them.

But I do have a tough story to tell that had to do with killing. My brother had a BB gun and sold it to me for $10. I was eleven or twelve and nearing the end of public school. We were at the farm, and I wanted to try it out, so I went down to the slough looking for something to shoot. I took a few aimless shots at a bottle and a tin can, missing both. Frustrated, I noticed a mother duck and a few ducklings. So, I shot at them. Surprisingly (and unfortunately), I hit one of the ducklings. Excited by my success, I kept shooting till I ran out of bullets. They all missed their target.

Victory Protocol 59: When passions and primitive views are in play, virtue declines.

When I was walking back to the house, I started to feel bad. I had killed that duckling for no reason, and all it showed was that my view of the world didn't extend beyond what I felt like doing. It was worse when I realized that the baby duck couldn't yet fly. By missing the mother, I demonstrated my lack of skill; by killing that duckling, I demonstrated my ignorance. Truly all suffering stems from obsession with one's own ego. Years later, I'd face this issue about killing again for sport. That would be the last time.

The summer before high school, these lessons about how I had developed my values, worldview, and self-identity were starting to come into focus, although I didn't know it at the time. I was at a point where I could become either an absolutist, striving for success and ego validation, or a humanist with a more global view.

The shadow holds those unnameable desires and fears, and its repression keeps the mainstream of society in the illusion of safety and control. In the positive, it probably prevents people from getting into trouble. But in the negative, it keeps us asleep and uncompassionate.

19. Extracurricular

Some experiences pushed me out of the archaic paradigm of the tribe and into the dynamic of the Psynauts. One of these was actually a missed experience. My brother-in-law was an Air Force wing commander and piloted F-14 fighter planes. Stationed in Moose Jaw, he lived just down the road. One summer day, he asked me if I'd like to go up with him in his jet. I almost fell out of myself with excitement. I waited all week for that Saturday morning, dreaming of flying and soaring in the air. But come Thursday evening, he called to say that one of the Air Force bigwigs from Ottawa was coming to town for a site inspection, and he wouldn't be able to take me up. Personally, I think my family got to him and kiboshed the idea. If we had gotten caught, he was probably looking at a court martial, and I am sure he had thought better of it. But still, so close!

Greed can be laced with adventure. At another time, my sister and her husband, the Air Force pilot, were stationed in Portage la Prairie in the Canadian Prairies. I was about ten and in a constant siege mentality with my parents. My sister, ten years older than me and just married, suggested I spend a week with them on the base. I jumped at the chance to get out of town, an ongoing theme in my story …

After I was there a few days, I organized two of the bigger local boys into a boxing match and rigged the fight as they were not so keen to punch each other. I suggested they pretend to hit each other hard and make lots of noise so it would sound believable, and we would charge all the other kids a dime (10 cents) to watch. We'd split the take: they'd get 50% (shared between them) and I'd get 50%. Since I was the brains of the outfit, and they were just going to pretend to fight, it seemed fair.

All was going according to plan. We had the fight set up for 3 p.m. the next day, and we had the promise of about twenty kids coming. We even had a few advanced sales pocketed, totalling about $0.50, when the parents found out. Drats, that was the end of that!

The two lessons learned here speak to Protocols 8.0, 8.1, and 8.2. The clinging to our desires feeds our self-image, which ends up having us pursuing fame and fearing shame, chasing gain and avoiding loss, seeking pleasure and avoiding pain, cherishing fame and denying blame.

Victory Protocol 60: The eight poisons are fame and shame, loss and gain, praise and blame, pleasure and pain.

After our thwarted match, I was noticeably less popular around the base than in the first few days when I was seen as friendly, funny, cute, charming, and energetic. My sister informed me, much to her embarrassment, that I had become devious, selfish, crafty, sly, and mean. From this story, I have no trouble seeing the charming, loving husband and father (or mother) that can become tied up in greed and ambition—the shadow sides of invention, imagination, and creation. The scale tips on the basis of motivation.

Women tend to get off lighter than they deserve on this point, and I wonder if it's just the difference between oxytocin and testosterone levels. Their tendency to be more connective and inter-referencing may hide their bouts of sociopathy better or perhaps make it less intense than men's. The exception is perhaps the threatened female; the old saw "Hell hath no fury like a woman scorned" isn't without some justification.

Our horizons get stretched in interesting ways, and mine were no exception. However, a few of my experiences were out of this world … and given my origins, may have been preordained.

20. Strange Tales

One of my favorite influences from this time was my aunt, a legal secretary who worked in Vancouver. She never married, and used her spare time and holidays to travel. I used to really look forward to her coming to town because she would talk about Africa and China and India. In retrospect she might have been a lesbian, or maybe she was just asexual. In any case, her sense of adventure and unconventional lifestyle were hugely formative. Maybe it's bred in the bone, to quote Robertson Davies, but my early days of venturing out reflected hers, a family thing. I remember thinking that when I grew up, I was going to be like her. I would go to all sorts of places and have all sorts of wild experiences—with elephants, fakirs, and strange and exotic people.

During one of my aunt's visits to town, I went to the movies with my friends. We got handed glasses to watch in 3D, which was a new thing then. It was a horror movie, and with the 3D glasses on, it really seemed like the monster was going to get you. At the end of the showing, the manager of the movie theater came out onstage and said, "Okay, boys and girls, as long as you're in this theater, you're safe. But whatever you do when you go home, do NOT turn out the lights in your bedroom when it is all dark and put on these glasses because the monster will come and get you." We kids giggled and laughed, thinking, "Yeah, sure, can't fool me, I'm not scared." Outwardly, we assured each other we would be trying it out that night just as soon as it got dark, and strutted off in all our glory.

After dinner, I went into my bedroom, turned off the lights, and held the glasses in my hand. And stood there. And continued to stand there. And stood there some more. Nope, wasn't going to do it. Feeling sheepish, I came out of my bedroom. My aunt happened to be standing in the hallway, so thinking myself very clever, I asked her if she would mind going into my room, closing the door, putting these glasses on, and then telling me what she saw. So, she did … but she didn't come out. I waited and waited, and finally, she came out after what seemed like hours but was probably only a few minutes. She looked very white and rattled. I asked her what she had seen, and she said, "I can't talk about it, but whatever you do, do NOT put these glasses on in that room in the dark."

Hopelessness

Ah, now you begin to understand
You can't escape me, you can't run,
You can't hide, you can't buy me,
You can't kill me, you can't scare me,
You can't evade me,
There's no place where I am not

I am devastation, destruction, dissolution
The end of time and the end of you

> *Give to me the timid and terrified*
> *Remember, I am Bhairava, lord of death*
> *I am Beezelbub, lord of dung*
> *I am Lucifer, lord of darkness after the light is distinguished*
>
> *Weep when you see me*
> *Your life as you know it is over*
> *I gather your bones and eat your flesh*
> *No one will know you, and none will remember you*

Although I was suspicious, I believed her enough to not put the glasses on that night. It took me three days to build up the courage to finally do it, and it changed my world forever in terms of understanding fear. But if you're reading this, I strongly recommend if you find yourself in a similar situation that you don't do it. Nope, don't go in the bedroom, don't turn off the lights, and definitely do NOT put on the 3D glasses. If you do, you'll never be the same again. Altered states are a game changer.

Altered states call to mind my first introduction to the drug LSD when I was around ten. My cousin was a psychiatric nurse at the Weyburn mental institution in Saskatchewan. She was visiting my mother, having tea as I walked in and sat down to say hello. My cousin had been recounting to my mother her experience volunteering to take LSD under clinical conditions in the Institute. She described it as terrifying and completely mind-bending, and she said she would never do it again. I remember thinking as she told her tale of horror and fear mixed with awe and amazement that it sounded just like my regular day. Do kids live on the liminal edges that we only lose as we get plaited into the status-quo-world of our parents and other adults?

Is the shock edge of hallucinatory experience just a reverberation out of the "normal" world relaxing into the "non-normal world?" Although my LSD trips were recreational, they pushed me out into the spiritual and perhaps the beginning of Psynaut awareness. (Certainly later, for others, ayahuasca and peyote-style vision quests that were conducted with some form and ritual seemed to make for easier passage between these realms.) Much later, when I discovered that Hwa Yen philosophy reported that the Buddha lived in all realms simultaneously, interpenetrating, without obstruction, and in a totality that embraced all of reality, it all made much more sense to me. It at least made the ongoing arguments between Plato and Aristotle, or faith and science, redundant.

The shock of an LSD trip to the ego is like breaking the sound barrier—strictly speaking, you don't have to do it, but then you don't get to see the stars up close. Personally, I think it's a bit like losing one's virginity because it opens up a whole new universe. It isn't required, but oh boy, what you're missing! LSD returns us to pure perception without the confusions of thinking and feeling (once their neurotic components have been dropped). However, having crossed the fear barrier a few times, doing it again gets repetitive. The meditative path takes you much further and deeper, as the drug limits consciousness rather than expanding it.

Victory Protocol 61: Psychic powers include first and foremost the ability to remain in a clear, blissful, loving state regardless of circumstances.

Altered realties were going to be part of my life. And they began with my mother.

This was not such a bad thing, since my mother was a psychic and had a great many of those experiences, some of which were documentable. This talent of my mother's, shared with her two sisters and their mother, was accepted as normal in our family. We got quite used to my mother's "outbreaks" accompanied by a minor swoon, then a vision and an energy rush. In a few minutes, she would calm down and give us the report, after which we'd go back to bed or go about the rest of our day.

My mother's psychic episodes were an initial indicator that my world was much larger than what appeared to my senses. In another era, she and her family would probably have been called witches or shamans. While they never had the mapping systems that Psynauts use, their experiences were on a similar psychic-phenomena plane. She and her witchy sisters and mother did automatic writing (channeling dead people onto paper) before they all got married. They kept pages and pages of notes until my sister got them.

I grew up with this psychic entertainment. This was before Netflix, YouTube, social media, and television with its 24/7 news channels drowning out almost everything really important. Don't get me wrong, I love all of these media … but as the Psynaut Paracelsus said, "The disease is in the dose, not the substance." In fact, I wasn't sure of the exact quote, but I looked it up online, and there it was. The Internet knows everything; it's a very handy resource.

From an early age, they practiced automatic writing. My aunt from Alaska acted as the medium, and her mother and her two sisters, including my mother, recorded the data. My earliest memory of this practice was when I was in high school, and my mother told me that my father's best friend had drowned in the farm slough (pond). They were about five years old, and all my father could do was watch, as he couldn't swim and there was nothing around to save the boy. The "witches" had pages and pages of automatic writings, and one of them was from this boy. He told my mother to tell Willis, my dad, to not be upset, that he was fine, and that it wasn't my father's fault. My mother had been dating my father at the time they channeled this boy but decided, probably wisely, to not tell my dad. Years later, after they were married, my mother told my father of their psychic ability. He turned to her and said, uncharacteristically, "Never speak of this again."

When my mother was recounting this to me, when I was a teenager, she said, "Don't mention it to your father; it will just upset him." But I needed to get to the bottom of it, so I went in the washroom while he was shaving and asked him if it was true. He, again uncharacteristically, ignored me completely, nicked himself shaving, and never said a word about it.

On another occasion, in 1964, there was a huge earthquake in Alaska where my aunt lived. Before anyone beyond the quake's reach knew about it, my mother woke up in the middle of the night, screaming and fretting. This was not unusual for us, so we all got out of bed as she went through her emotions, and eventually, she calmed down, went quiet, and said, "It's okay, I'm going back to bed." We asked her what had happened, and she said that there had been a large earthquake in Alaska, that her sister's house had been destroyed, but that they were all okay. She went back to bed and slept well, but we were up for a couple of hours due to the energy in the room.

The next day, the earthquake was all over the news, and my mother was getting phone calls right and left from friends worrying about my aunt and her family. My mother assured them that they were all fine even though their house had been destroyed. At the time, getting information took a lot longer, so it was a couple of days before telephone lines were working again and my aunt could call to let us know that in fact her home had been destroyed but the family was fine.

In yet another instance, I was traveling in a group in India when I was eighteen. We were sleeping in the Khyber Pass and were attacked by bandits. They were armed and vicious, but luckily no one was hurt, although we did get robbed and slapped around a little—probably just to dissuade us from fighting back, but since they had guns, we were unlikely to try. It was the first week of October 1970. I had been traveling for several months, and I wouldn't be returning to my parents' home for another ten months. After I returned, one day my mother and I were sitting on the porch having a cup of coffee when she turned to me and said, "So, you almost got killed by bandits in India in October, didn't you?"

My sister and I also had a certain amount of psychic ability. One evening, she borrowed all the automatic writings. Her husband was an Air Force pilot, as I've mentioned, and was flying night exercises while she was home alone reading the notes. She looked up from her bed, and there was a ghost (for lack of a better word) in the form of a man standing at the foot of it. She freaked out, said the Lord's prayer, and burned all the notes. I never got to read them in that form (see Protocols 4 and 4.1).

It turned out that my mother had had a similar experience when she was a young girl. She was visiting a friend of East Indian descent, heading up the stairs to join her friend on the second floor. As she was climbing, she saw the ghost of a man dressed in a kurta pajama and a turban, smiling at her. This freaked her out so much that she left the house and would never go back inside again.

This is the problem with having psychic ability without philosophical grounding—my mother would see things in terms of good and evil based on her religious and cultural bias. She was probably meeting the family's guru, and maybe it was the same ghost my sister saw because hers was also dressed in ethnic Indian wear.

My mother's psychic ability backfired on her as she got older because she couldn't separate actual physical phenomena from her psychic interpretive neuroses. Case in point: she told me one day that she was being chased by three Black men whom she saw downstairs from her apartment because they knew she knew that they were dealing drugs. I asked her how she was sure. She said because she saw them being chased last night by the police and there was gunfire, but they got away, and now they were here to get her because she had witnessed it all. I thought this was very unlikely and presumed she had seen something on TV that she got scrambled up with men downstairs.

The next day, I was at my mother's apartment. Three Black men were downstairs, and she pointed them out to me to prove her case. I went downstairs, introduced myself to the three men, and asked how they were doing. They were very friendly and explained that one of them and his wife were renting an apartment in the building and that the other two were her brothers. So, he was just showing them around. I found out later that day that there had been a cop show on TV wherein some Black men who were dealing drugs had been chased by cops. My mother's confusion was that she could not separate one story from the other in her mind because her right brain fluidity, at least in this part of her life, didn't recognize boundaries. I expect this is one of the reasons why her psychic ability worked the way it did, but it didn't do her any favors emotionally or psychologically, as she would get not only deep insights but also delusional stories from her conditioned personal life.

I told her who the Black men were and even took her downstairs to meet them. She was very friendly, but I saw the tears in her eyes. Soon after, I asked her about her psychic phenomena, and she replied that she had shut it down. She said the incident with the three Black men had shown her that it was no longer useful and even problematic. I told her this is why one meditates and pursues the spiritual life, especially one with a good discipline and clear boundaries—so that we can train ourselves to make the distinctions she was confused by. At this point in her life, she wasn't ready to hear that most of what she had experienced some meditators spend years on the cushion trying to contact. She would come to this at the end of her life, on her deathbed. In the last week of her life, as I was sitting with her in the nursing home, she said to me, "You are calm, aren't you?" I said yes. She asked, "And you're at peace?" I said yes again, and she said, "So this is what you've been doing all these years?" Once more I said yes. And she said, "I get it now."

Victory Protocol 61.1 (variant): Other psychic powers can include the ability to read minds, being able to hear what is not said, recollection of previous lives, knowing other people's karma, and the ability to travel out of body.

Obviously, these revolve around the realms-within-realms idea, and their accesses are trans-physical but not trans-material (that is, material density, like air, is different from physical density, like bone). Mirrors are often used to demonstrate this distinction; the image in a mirror is identical to the physical image in front of it, but the object in front of a mirror need not be physical. It could be just light (not dark). These powers are, in that sense, trans-sensual. Perhaps the example of memory helps: one can remember one's house and see it clearly without being actually in it. Also, a room of mirrors (eight sides) can reflect countless images at the same time, all in the same space, without obstruction, simultaneously arising and interpenetrating. As the Psynaut Shakespeare said, "There are more things in heaven and earth, than are dreamt of in your philosophy, Horatio."

In meditation retreats, all sorts of strange phenomena may occur, and after the initial surprise, the meditator starts to integrate them seamlessly into their experience. Psynauts tend not to make a big deal out of all this, as it can be a serious distraction from entering our guild. In any case, such phenomena don't amount to much, as my mother's experiences show.

21. High School,
Pre-Driving License

Years later, after I had learned more about karma (VP 3, 3.1) and changed my errant ways, I reflected on what had instigated or supported the change. I concluded that looking for happiness where it couldn't be found, namely, in a contented and satisfied "self," was the source of my discontent. In fact, the error is in the very idea of a "self" (VP 9s).

The self looks to such things as material objects, interpersonal relationships, and careers, subject as they are to the whims of our personalities and uncontrollable world events, to find happiness. Occasionally, we can even find happiness in them; often, we can't. But then we miss the next point of this self problem: it's never satisfied for long! The nature of the self is to be discontented, regularly seeking its paradise lost. This is the essence of the Psynaut program: finding paradise again. In the meantime, the ego builds its refuge in houses of cards.

My mother, my father, my brother, and my sister all went to the same high school. My parents were born around 1905, and my brother finished high school in 1963, so the school had been around a long time, at least by North American standards. But when my turn came, they had just built a new high school, so in 1963, as I was entering grade 9, we became the first full class to go through the new school, graduating in 1967. That meant that all the students coming to the new high school were drawn from quite a few different junior high schools. It was a melting pot of neighborhoods and school cultures. But since the Prairies can be very monoculture both in terms of crops and people, it wasn't until grade 9 that I knowingly met my first Jew, and I didn't meet a Black person until I was eighteen!

I was fourteen in grade 9, and it was a big year for my education. I was introduced to French, which made no sense to me, not least of which since there wasn't a French-speaking person within 1,000 miles as far as I knew. We boys had shop (metal, electric, carpentry, auto) while the girls had home economics (cooking, sewing)—one had to stay in their gender slot. There was also gym class that included gymnastics and dancing. We had a dress code and behavior standards that could get you kicked out if you pushed too hard. It was a father-knows-best kind of world.

Jockeying for position, a teenage rite of passage, occupied a great deal of time. If you were from my town, you had to fight occasionally. You didn't have to win; you just needed to stand in. Fights also got much more significant. My two primary school pugilistic contests were short and mild, but high school was a more vicious game. One boy and I got into it for the stupidest reason. I had lent him a quarter that he refused to pay back, and I challenged him a few times to return it, which he refused. So, the fight was on for after school, and a bunch of students gathered to watch the event. I must have forgotten my early childhood management skills as I didn't arrange for someone else to fight for me. I guess it was a matter of saving face or pride, not wanting to be taken advantage of. Here again was a life lesson on how our consciousness is trapped by our views and emotions.

I started out pretending I was Muhammad Ali, and he came in like a berserker, flailing his arms and kicking and biting. Where did he learn to do that? That wasn't in any movie I ever saw, wherein the hero gentlemanly beats up the bad guy. My Queensbury rules weren't working, so I reverted to what I'm better at, which is wrestling. I grabbed him around the neck, threw him over my shoulder, landed on top of him in a neck lock, and proceeded to punch him in the face a few times. At that moment, the whole thing seemed stupid to me, and all the energy and enthusiasm I'd had for it dissolved. I asked him if he had had enough, and he said, "If you have," and so we called it quits. We stood up awkwardly and kind of shook hands, embarrassed by our antics. We were distantly polite to each other after that, but limits and boundaries had been established.

This is what every soldier needs to know when he goes into battle: whether the guy beside him is reliable. Whether or not he'll have his back, and not be a bigger risk to his life when it comes down to it. This is why boys probably test each other in different ways than girls do. I've only witnessed two girls' fights, and they were much more vicious and terrifying than the boys' fights even though they didn't do as much damage. I think it was because there was so much emotion and vindictiveness in their battle whereas—from my experience, anyway—boy fights were more of a test. Losing wasn't the main issue; the central point was whether you could be reliable even though we didn't know it at the time. In my day, fights ended as soon as it was clear who had won and that the loser had not caved.

I returned home from my schoolyard fight covered in blood and sporting a black eye and a swollen cheek. I was met by my brother-in-law, the Air Force pilot, who decided to offer me boxing lessons (which were appreciated, but then, he hadn't met the berserker). Once he realized it was my opponent's blood and not my own, he said I didn't need his help.

The boy and I saw each other the next day at school. We each carried our marks of combat, and the other students who noticed gave us a certain kind of respect. After that, I decided that if I was going to fight any more battles, they were going to be on my terms.

(The first thing the Americans did when they invaded Afghanistan was to secure the oil fields. So much for the fight against terrorism, which they had helped create in the first place. There was an argument going around at the time that since the Americans had a tested army in combat from being in Vietnam, Russia needed its own version, thus, Afghanistan. Was the oil an afterthought? Probably not, as Chechnya is on the pipeline from Afghanistan to Russia. War is always about wealth; power is secondary, and doctrine is smoke. And given the EOEI—energy out, energy in—for oil, we can see why everyone fights over it.)

Trying to fit in and behave the way you're expected to is tough since it is all unconsciously learned and often not stated. For instance, my brother-in-law expected me to fight, but no one would ever say so outright. The girl that had gotten pregnant was supposed to, but not at that time. Our most pernicious behaviors are learned.

Victory Protocol 62: The four obscurations are ignorance, habit, conflicting emotions, and negative actions.

In this case, ignorance doesn't mean being stupid or not knowing something; it's about not looking. Not seeing things as they are but as how we'd like them to be, or seeing things as they are not, to reinforce bias. Habits keep us asleep. True, they save time and energy by automating our actions, but they also dampen creativity and imagination. Negative actions and emotions, obscure our freedom.

We had a neighbor kid my age whose father was the local Mafia gangster. He had three daughters plus my friend, who was the youngest in the family. Gordon was a bit of an oddball, not that we all weren't. He was big, not the brightest, but friendly in a way that no one really warmed up to. Being an outsider myself, we were sort of friends. We would occasionally play over at his house, and a few of those times are particularly strong in my memory. The first was because of his three gorgeous sisters. They were only one year apart from each other in age, but were older than us. That made them sixteen, seventeen, and eighteen. They had this habit of walking around the house mostly naked! The oldest two definitely seemed to know what they were doing. They would walk by Gordon and me, coming out of the shower with a towel or going into the bathroom in their underwear, and not be particularly careful about what got revealed in the process.

For a fourteen-year-old boy like myself, playing with Gordon was a mixed bag. While I was not super fond of him, I did have quite a strong attraction to his sisters who ignored us completely because we were a couple of years younger than them. The highlight was when the eighteen-year-old came out of the bathroom from having a shower. Completely naked, she leaned over the upstairs railing and asked Gordon to bring her underwear from the downstairs dryer. Stunned, I just stared. She looked at me as if I were invisible, turned around, and walked into her room. Shortly after this incident, the nudity ended, at least when I was around. But Gordon said it was still commonplace when they were alone.

His father was into gaming, drugs, and prostitution. It came as no surprise when one day Gordon told me his father had $10,000 stashed in the downstairs freezer. Gordon was an inveterate liar, so I didn't believe him and asked him to prove it. He took me downstairs, opened the freezer, and pulled out three or four plastic bags filled with $20 bills. He suggested we take some of it and insisted it would never be missed. With an intelligence that I have no reason to claim, I said no.

The same day, we needed a saw to cut something; I don't remember what. He challenged me to cut his arm with the saw and kept saying I couldn't manage it. I didn't think it was a particularly crazy idea at the time—it was just the sort of idiocy that young boys would get up to.

After being challenged a couple of times, I said OKAY and cut him a little bit, just enough to break the skin. He couldn't believe I had gone through with it. I learned a big lesson here: the need for attention can go to very large extremes, and if you can't get it by being good, or by being bad, you'll get it by being crazy. I don't know how Gordon turned out in the end, as I lost contact with him after I left town for university, around the same time his father went to jail. But I have a sinking feeling that his ending wasn't great.

The third incident took place a year or two later. Our local summer exhibition had horse races, and one day when I was with some friends, Gordon showed up. In an effort to win favor, he told us which horse to bet on in the last race of the day. He told us that this was how they laundered the money from his father's activities, that this particular race was fixed, and that the horse with 19-to-1 odds would win. Since he was such a big liar, we were not usually prone to believe him, but given that his father was the local gangster, we did in this case. My two friends decided not to follow his advice, but I took a calculated gamble and placed three of my precious $5 bills on his horse.

At the beginning of the race, my friends were teasing me for being an idiot as the horse was running last. But magically, it came from behind and won by a nose, giving me $60 which at the time was a fortune for me. I had to hide that money as I had no way to account for it, and in those days, spending it on something I'd then have to bring home would draw attention.

Gordon showed up after the race and asked us if we had bet on the nag. I said I had, and he asked me how much I had won. When I told him, he claimed I owed him $20 for providing me with the winner. When I didn't want to give him the money, he suggested his older brother could change my mind for me, so I gave him the twenty bucks. Ahhhhh greed, how insidious. (See VP 40.)

There was a girl, Marlene, who lived across the street whom I found very attractive. She was a year or so older than me. My bedroom looked onto her bedroom, but while I was on the ground floor, she was on the second floor. We kissed and made out a few times, but she had an older boyfriend who had a car, and she told me she was having sex with him. Having sex was the holy grail, but on the other hand, I probably wasn't quite sure what that meant exactly, and I couldn't understand why she didn't want to share with me too. But one cannot underestimate what fourteen-year-olds don't understand!

At night, I would sometimes look out my window in the hopes of seeing her in hers, and I told her this. She joined me after that and said she enjoyed it. Occasionally she would come to the window after having a shower, but since the angle from lower floor to upper floor only allowed me to see her shoulders, it was a bit frustrating. She didn't say anything when I told her this, but a few days later when I managed to catch her at her window, my view had changed to the waist up. I guess she was standing on something. Seeing her naked torso and her beautiful breasts sent shivers through my body. She waved, smiled, and disappeared.

This was the beginning of the end of my virginity since occasionally after that, we would get topless and fondle each other while passionately making out in either her bedroom or mine. How this escaped our parents I have no idea. But at this point, parents were merely a resource delivery system, and it didn't feel like they had any context for our personal lives at all.

In grade 9 my interests, and those of almost all the boys around me, turned more and more to girls, and we entered new territory. For instance, all the pretty girls in our grade or above had no time for us, so we turned our attention to girls in grades 7 and 8. This is a very interesting social phenomenon which would later be termed hypogamy and hypergamy, but at that time, it was just the lay of the land. For instance, Marlene from across the street "dumped me" for the boy two grades up who also had a car.

There are good reasons for this phenomenon. Girls mature faster than boys, but why? It seems to me that because girls can get pregnant and have babies as soon as they begin to menstruate, nature has built in a "selfish gene" to protect them. Insofar as we are creatures of nature, we live by this programming. It is probably the basis for things like monogamy and pair bonding that protect the woman from unwanted suitors but may also exclude the best suitor.

Therefore, there is an argument for hypogamy which in the vernacular of day-to-day life could be translated as an upgrade. It could also be because girls' brains at rest are busier than boys' brains when they are active and that the corpus callosum, the bridge between the hemispheres of our brain, is bigger and far more active in girls than in boys. If we want to keep it simple and get things done, boys might have the advantage. But if we need to find something in the fridge, don't send the guy—he'll just see the beer.

With the advent of feminism that included women's suffrage, career equality (principally in terms of economic freedom), and birth control, women have been liberated to seek their own best interest without having to rely on a man. The sexual revolution of the 1960s was likely a first forage into new territory in terms of relationships between the sexes.

I also had a crush on a girl in my grade 9 class. She had a boyfriend who let me know in no uncertain terms to leave her alone. Since she was a bit scary anyway, thirteen going on thirty, I admired her from a distance. Unfortunately for me, she got pregnant halfway through the year and was whisked away from school. This was the second time a girl I knew had disappeared for being pregnant. Is it any wonder we have such weird sexual attitudes and behaviors when life in the raw needs to be put in the shadow, hidden away, and made to be shameful? Granted, it was probably not her desired outcome, being thirteen years old, but I felt we could have done better. What is more disturbing is that no one questioned it, no one offered an alternative, and no one thought of the implications of our attitudes about sex. This was just five years after Elvis had gotten arrested for wiggling his hips!

Being thirteen and sexually "mature," I approached masturbation with a vengeance. It became an all-consuming activity and was far more interesting to me than school. When it came to girls, though, I had a language problem—I couldn't seem to translate my sexual vibrancy into a language that girls wanted to entertain. But perseverance furthers, as the I Ching says, so the problem was remedied a couple of years later.

I was not a kid and not yet an adult—strange years, teenage ones. As insurance companies and construction sites know, people under twenty-five, especially men, are far more prone to accidents, largely because they are testing their limits and think they're invulnerable. It doesn't help that the brain is going through a major re-fit during those years. Some think that mental functions like organization, empathy, and guilt are underused during this time. From the adult point of view, teenagers are just crazy. As I remember it, the drive was to test your limits. Obviously, this could be a two-edged sword.

Like I said, I didn't really enjoy school. I was a social misfit, and I was not the best student. I managed to pass from year to year, but barely.

There were a few exceptions, however. I wrote a short story for my grade 9 English class that involved the protagonist getting into a predicament that was impossible to get out of. I showed it to my older sister who said, "Elbud, this is impossible, there's no way out of this." I went to a higher authority, my parents, who both said, "Impossible." I was too lazy to start over, so I just made it into a dream and had the hero wake up!

I did love history though, and math. I saw history as a late-night movie with battles, plots, scheming, and movement of people through the different eras as an epic story. Math I loved for its beauty. Such an elegant and precise language for the measure of things. I learned later in university that math majors also tended to do well in philosophy. And that's where I ended up at the end of my university career: math and philosophy.

High school itself left few impressions before I could drive. Getting a driving license at sixteen was freedom on another level than bike riding …

22. High School,
Post-Driving License

As I've told you, I learned to drive young. So, by the time it came to take my exam, I was already a competent driver (actually, better than competent). My brother-in-law would take me out to a snow-covered parking lot in a mall after hours and have me race across it, then crank the wheel to go into a 360-degree spin and other fancy stuff, all before I was fifteen. I got my learner's permit on my birthday but had to wait a week to take the written test. When I asked why I had to wait, the lady looked at me and with a wry smile said, "You're not supposed to know how to drive yet, you're supposed to be just learning."

I replied, "I'm a farm kid, we all know how to drive by the time we're ten!"

I was exaggerating a bit, but she laughed and commented, "Maybe so, but you don't drive tractors on city streets."

The following week, I took my exam. The examiner failed me. I said, "Hold on, what did I get wrong?"

He laughed. "Nothing."

"Then why did you fail me?" I growled.

"You're not supposed to know how to drive this well on your sixteenth birthday. I'm slowing you down."

He had a point. One Saturday night two years previously, while my parents were out playing bridge, my friends and I stole my dad's company car and took it for a joy ride. We faithfully returned it, parking it in the driveway and feeling quite proud of ourselves … until my friend pointed out that the car had been on the street when we took it! Panicking, as they were due home any moment, I jumped in the car and proceeded to back out but didn't close the car door completely. It swung open and pinned my friend's arm to the wall of the house. Luckily his arm was okay, but the car door was bent and the siding ripped up.

Abandoning all, I ran into my bedroom and crawled under the bed, fearing the wrath of Dad (who might as well have been God). This was a little surprising in retrospect because Mom was usually the more wrathful. I only ever saw my father lose his temper twice and drunk only once.

When he came into the bedroom, he asked, "What are you doing under the bed?"

I answered, "Avoiding getting hit. I'll pay for the damages, and I'm sorry."

He silently left the room. I did eventually pay him back through cutting the lawn in the summer and shoveling snow in the winter.

Victory Protocol 63: Four kinds of neuroses can manifest in children stemming from negative shaping: the hurt child, the critical child, the angry child, and the guilty child.

We tend to grow up and embody one of these children—often all of them, but predominately only one—when we are in unpleasant states. For me, it was the hurt child. As adults, this embodiment will show up at work or in our personal relationships. Not recognizing which child is present, we can project our frustrations out on ourselves or others as reasons for our unhappiness, and miss the child in it altogether.

Another way of seeing this is an aspect of suffering. We seek to avoid unhappiness or seek happiness in three ways. One, we move towards objects, trying to possess them and gain security. Two, we try to push against objects, trying to protect and insulate ourselves. Three, we try to avoid choices, running away from intense feelings.

Victory Protocol 8.4 (variant): Greed = moving towards. Hate = moving against. Confusion = moving away.

The next year, I was in grade 11. I was sixteen and now had my driver's license. My father had bought a new car with the idea that the old one would become my mother's car to go grocery shopping and run errands, but in fact it turned out to be mostly mine. And with the advent of the car came the first real girlfriend. I'm not implying a cause-and-effect relationship, but the fact of the matter is they did coincide pretty closely.

I learned a lesson about managing my time early on with the car. In the morning, I would drive to school, and at lunchtime, I'd drive home. I gave a ride to my girlfriend and my best friend. They were to be in the car five minutes after the bell, or I'd leave them behind. And I did leave them behind a few times. It took me twenty minutes to drive each of them home and get back to my house, then twenty minutes to eat, and twenty minutes go back and get each of them to return to school on time.

Victory Protocol 64: If you have the responsibility, you must have the authority. If you have the authority, you must be responsible.

And with the car and the girlfriend came "parking." Our first sex happened in the backseat of that old 1959 Chevy. I was sixteen, she was fifteen, and neither of us was really prepared for the fact that sex was a completely different ball game than say baseball or hockey.

Debbie and I first met at our local church—some sort of "youth night" in which neither of us was much interested. But we were interested in each other. That was a year earlier, and although I'd walk her home and we would kiss and I would try and fondle her breasts, we weren't prepared to do more in public. With my access to an automobile, we at last had some privacy.

Everybody watches cop shows, and coming out of the United States, they're all very gritty and hard. But one winter's evening as Debbie and I were making love in the backseat of the Chevy, our pants around our ankles and her top and bra around her neck, we were surprised by a knock on the windshield. Getting caught in this compromising position curiously didn't cause either of us much embarrassment, but the cop did tell us to stop and get out of there.

We didn't learn our lesson because the following year at my high school graduation party, Debbie and I couldn't find a place to make love, so once more we found ourselves in the car in an identical position. And once more, we had a knock on the windshield, only this time it was from a concerned passerby. Our windows were rolled up, and the engine was on to protect us from the cold, so he was worried we might asphyxiate ourselves and suggested we open the window a little. We did, he left, and we carried on.

Debbie's family were socialists (for the American readers, that does not mean communists), and my family were liberals (for the American readers, that means Democrats). Her father and I would get into arguments about this. He told me that arguing with me was like arguing with a brick wall. (Years later, when I knew something about astrology, I had an explanation for this: Mars in Gemini.) One evening during a heated argument, he suggested I go home because I might regret what I might say. Later as he was seeing me out the door and I was waving to Debbie, he laughed and said, "Elbud, when you get older, you're going to be a socialist." And as it turns out, he was right.

Occasionally, I would sneak into Debbie's bedroom, which was in the basement of their house, and spend the night. I would leave my house around 11 p.m. when everyone had retired, drive over to Debbie's, and crawl through the bedroom window and into her bed. We would make love and fall asleep. But I would wake before dawn, sneak back out the window, return to my house, climb through my window, and look like I had been there all night.

One morning however, her father saw me climb out her window, get into my car, and drive off. He called my parents and ratted me out. Adults were so paralyzed about sexuality in those days. Not much was said, but I got grounded. I wasn't supposed to go out for a week or see Debbie at all. I didn't stick to either of those terms, but that was the last time I snuck into Debbie's bedroom. Instead, we had sex in my bedroom when my parents were out, but mostly it was in the car. Luckily, she never got pregnant. I used the withdrawal method—not very reliable, and even less satisfying, but we got away with it.

When things don't happen that you might expect but that nevertheless you ignore, thinking "It'll never happen to me," there's an underlying substrate that makes you feel you've dodged something ...

Oblivion

Now you are mine
I am your hopes and fears
Often switching them so you are confused
I am the enemy
Cry now, I am the end and the beginning

I offer you your dreams, your house,
And your children
Your money, your fortune, and
I will take them away
I am death, I am disappointment and despair,
I am lost hope, I am the drama of searching
And the tragedy that takes it away

Your pleasure and your projects
I consume and serve back to you
As trauma, hurt, and pain

I offer you hope and promise,
I sell it in packages
And advertise it on the Internet
On television and the media
Better buy it now

I never wanted to get married, nor have children. A woman told me years later that she thought a woman didn't get pregnant if the man didn't have at least an unconscious wish for it. Her theory was that the female unconsciously "blocked" it if the "support" wasn't there. I never gave the theory much credence. Another friend of mine told me she and her husband had conceived while they were practicing three different kinds of birth control! It's hard to say if there are any rules.

(Many years later, as a farm wife, Debbie had three daughters, so it wasn't that she couldn't. Maybe it was me. Since I didn't go on to have any children this time around as a Psynaut on Earth, it might indeed have been me.)

Debbie had an older sister whose boyfriend was a friend of mine. In the summer, Debbie and her sister took the older sister's car and drove out to Banff. Her boyfriend, my friend, didn't have a car but suggested we take mine to drive out there and meet them. On the way, my car was leaking oil pretty badly, so we replaced the head gasket in the campground as my friend was handy with cars. You can't do this anymore with new cars—in those days, everyone got a little bit handy at everything, as parts were still mechanical and accessible, but they have become so complicated now with electronics that you need a specialist almost to open a door.

Once we arrived at the campground, we found Debbie and her sister, and from there the waters divided. Debbie and I shared one tent, and her sister and my friend shared another. The four of us spent a very enjoyable few days before we had to return for summer jobs.

Given our sanitation conditions in the tent, we decided to buy some condoms. In those days, you had to ask a pharmacist for condoms; they weren't on the shelf. When we asked for a pack, the pharmacist asked, "Are you married?" Stunned, we said no, so he sent us away along with a stern look and a disgusted frown.

Debbie was my girlfriend for three years in high school. We broke up once because she went on a date with another guy, which was fair enough looking back at it. But from my perspective then, I didn't like it.

Victory Protocol 65: Anger, pride, passion, jealousy, and stupidity are hindrances.

How many of our insecurities are built around a presumed hurt (see VP 15)? We equate love with some kind of exclusivity when in fact exclusivity is mostly about fear of abandonment or rejection. We've made "ownership" equivalent to commitment or integrity. Religion does this to help keep workers in the fields. And perhaps to keep us from killing each other. Anyway, the breakup was short, as Debbie and I had a deep interest in each other.

Years later, after Debbie was married with children, we met for coffee on her farm. It was a pleasant meeting—I still had fond feelings for her, and I guess she did for me. She suggested that we have sex again as she wanted to know what it was like now that she, and I, were more mature. I feel bad that I turned her down because her request was only fair; she had been "ravaged" by young male testosterone and now, probably being more fully in the game, wanted to see how it would feel with her first lover.

But she was married, and I had just become a Buddhist and had some precepts to follow. That was the last time I saw her. She still occasionally comes to mind, and I think of her with fondness and care, and hope she is happy. I also hope she feels the same way towards me, but of this I will never be sure.

A story that sums up my obsession with girls took place in my last year of high school. We were playing football for the city championship in the stadium used for the professional games. We were playing against Balfour Tech, the high school that produced auto mechanics, carpenters, plumbers, electricians, and heavy-duty mechanics—basically, tough guys. There would be occasional gang fights between the regional high schools, but no one messed with Balfour.

Our school was in the suburbs, the home of managers, store owners, and higher-level bureaucrats. They were ahead by 6 points (21 to 15) in the 4th quarter, with only a minute remaining. I played both offense halfback and defensive safety, depending on the situation. But since I was the fastest man on the team, I was playing both positions during the last few minutes. The second-to-last play of the game had us on their 25-yard line with a 3rd and 10 situation. In other words, do or die. Our quarterback threw a little dump pass over the line of scrimmage to me, and I managed to run it into the end zone for the touchdown. We scored the extra point on the kick and were now ahead by one point with only one play remaining, the kickoff. My job as safety was to remain back in case their runner got through everyone else, thus the name "safety". Given it was the last play of the game, this was unlikely.

Our guy kicked off, and everybody went rushing down the field. A very beautiful young woman happened to be walking by the sidelines, and my attention went to her. She seemed to notice because she turned and smiled, which captured my attention even more, and I just had time to see their runner with the ball skirting past me. I took chase but to no avail. I did manage to catch his heel and trip him, but he fell right into the end zone, and they won the game. Not my best moment.

Like most teenagers, it was not in my range to merely be told what to think. So, when a particular high school teacher in grade 12 history grew tired of me arguing and challenging his social and political positions, plus others that were outside the history curriculum, he put me on the spot. If I wanted so much attention, he said, I could do a book report on *The Iliad*.

I presume he never thought I'd read it, but I did. Not that I exactly followed it. On the appointed day, he asked me if I'd read it and if I was ready to give a report. To everyone's surprise, I stood up and delivered it. But trying to explain *The Iliad* took more time than either of us had thought, occupying an entire class period. I left a few minutes at the end for questions, but not surprisingly, there were none. I think my jumbled report of the epic poem had dulled everybody into a stupor and perhaps with some amazement that I could go on for so long.

It was one of the last classes of the year, and nobody much cared. To my surprise, I had found *The Iliad* interesting. It had occupied my mind in a way the standard history classes had left numb even though I had always enjoyed history. I treated it like a late-night movie, an adventure story.

At the end of grade 11, the idea of what happens after high school loomed, and I knew I didn't want to go to work. I wasn't particularly interested in a trade, which left university. That meant I'd have to study hard the last year of high school if I wanted to continue my academic education, and I did. I was not a natural student, so it didn't come easy; I had to work for it. On my finals, I got six As, two Bs, and a D (you guessed it—French, which I think they sort of gave me). Some of the teachers spent the year trying to figure out how I was cheating, but motivation and aspiration are powerful forces, and if they are combined with effort, success is far more likely. After I got into university, however, I went back to Ds.

By the end of high school, I had sorted out my personality quirks enough to more or less fit in. Life seemed predictable and stable, but that shows you how foolish you can be. I thought myself pretty clever; I had just enrolled in university, I had managed to get a schedule without a single class starting before 10 a.m., and I had Fridays off. All was right with the world.

23. Leaving Town

One day in late September, I came home from university for lunch at noon (it was a five-minute walk), and my father presented me with unexpected news. He had been transferred to Ottawa and would be moving there with my mother the following spring, leaving me with three options. One, I could stay in Saskatoon to finish the year and move to Ottawa the next year. Two, I could just stay in Saskatoon and either live with my brother or on my own. Three, I could leave for Ottawa right away before enrollment closed at Carleton.

I asked him when the last day for registration was, and he said Friday. It was Wednesday. I had exactly one hour to decide, as Thursday would be a traveling day, and I'd have to withdraw from the university that very afternoon.

I remember going to my room, lying on my bed, and thinking about it. Since I had never been east of Winnipeg, I said yes to door number three. Wednesday afternoon, I withdrew from the university, and that night, we had a big party—so big in fact that I forgot to go home and pack. This was before cell phones, so my parents had had no way to get hold of me.

I arrived at the airport twenty minutes before my flight with five of my friends in the car including my girlfriend. We were all either still drunk, or severely hungover. My mother, God bless her soul, had packed my bags and met us there. As I climbed the stairs to the plane, weaving a little, I turned and waved at my friends and parents, unaware that except for a summer visit the following year, that part of my life was over forever. Even the person who returned the following summer was radically different from the one who was entering the plane. It was also my first time on a plane, and somehow that departure marked a death. Gone was Elbud of Saskatchewan. Who was going to emerge remained to be seen. But that decision to move for a new adventure was unconsciously setting the steps in motion to meet the path of the Psynaut I was to become. The big question around this age is twofold: who are you going to be (debating options), and how are you going to get there (via what catalysts)?

Victory Protocol 66: The question is not "to be or not to be;" the question is "what to be?"

Since I had never really fit in, I knew I needed to be something else. Could I do it from here, where I stood? Or did I need to change the room to change the contents? That was the debate; the catalyst was moving me. Remaining in Saskatoon, I would have stayed asleep.

Many years later, I had two students who were originally from India and who now lived in Saskatoon. Turns out that while my going to India opened a spiritual door for me, theirs got opened when they moved to Saskatoon from Mumbai!

***

Here ends the first volume of my journal. After many years, we Psynauts have discovered that the transition phase into "alienhood" requires stepping away before one can move forward again—like phases of the moon perhaps, or the seasons. Newcomers often get excited by the so-called spiritual life, and if they pick it up seriously, they can get tunnel-visioned. This can lead to what is called spiritual bypassing, so we either send them away for a while, or we go away for a time.

In that window, the student and the Psynaut get to reflect and see how determined (needy) the adept may be. If it is a casual interest, we might not see them again, or only sporadically. But if the drive is strong, they'll find their way back to us. Eventually, in the great arc of time, everyone moves forward into the land of unfolding we represent.

So, dear reader, off you go. May your journey lead you to happiness and contentment. May your suffering, and struggle, be large enough to keep you awake. Perhaps we'll meet again. If you are interested in pursuing the Psynaut vision, trust in the process. The Universe is always moving toward ever-evolving consciousness, and all you need to do is agree … and make the effort.

Having said that, there are two more volumes of this journal to be discovered—look to the concept of "mentor" for a clue to the next adventure. And, there are in fact more Victory Protocols to learn. Happy searching, Earthlings.

24. Kasya Reflects

Kasya set the journal down. He knew it was coming to an end given the few pages remaining, but he did not expect it to end this way. By now it was late morning, and he had run out of wood and food. He had a little water left, so he put his things together and headed down the mountain.

He had to trudge through the snow, but the morning sun was warm, and the sparkling light in the snow crystals made the day vibrant. Kasya walked and slid down the slopes in a daze. What now? He'd taken the journal with him but was not exactly sure what he would do with it ... make it public? Was that Avalokana's intention?

Kasya felt he'd entered a new stage in his life but had no words for it yet. He was about to find out that there were at least two sides to this saga. There was truth in every story, but it would take Kasya quite some time and a lot of tough changes before he came to realize that it was futile to seek only one correct perception because there were in fact at least ten perspectives.

Late in the day, Kasya stumbled into a local Kathmandu café. While devouring two meals and a few beers, he noticed what he knew to be a Buddhist monk, probably originally from Tibet, sitting in his maroon robes at the back of the café. The Tibetans had been overtaken by the "great reforming" Chinese who had replaced their primitive nomadic drudgery of watching yaks with the privilege of long hours and bad conditions in modern Chinese-owned factories.

The monk smiled and waved his mala (rosary) vaguely in Kasya's direction in an invitation to join him. So, Kasya did. As he sat down, the monk said in perfect English, "You look like you've had an adventure, and it's just beginning, yes?"

Surprised, Kasya asked the monk, "How did you know?"

The monk smiled and replied, "I've seen that look before, and it doesn't appear on Muggles."

Kasya was startled to hear a Tibetan monk reference Harry Potter, but before he could ask about it, the monk continued, "Except that Muggles have no magic, and we know of course that almost everyone has the capability; they just don't look for it or recognize it when it hits them in the face."

Leaving a stunned look on Kasya's face, the scraping of his chair could be heard as the monk stood up and said, "Well, I must be off. Good luck, young man, and as the famous sage once said, 'The journey of 1,000 miles begins with one step,' and one way or another, you've stepped onto that road." Chuckling, he added, "Or cliff—whichever."

The monk smiled at Kasya, rapped him gently on his head with his beads, and walked out.

Kasya sat there, shaken. Here was someone who had a better idea of what was going on in his life than he did. An unformed and silent moment vibrated in the back of his mind ...

Surrender

You can run, you can hide
You can bury yourself in appetite
The rap of my knuckles will shock and maybe hurt
Give it up
You can't win

Come to me, be my slave
I'll show you what you don't want to know
You're mine no matter what
Agony, loneliness, worry,
And trauma
These are my tools

Kasya replayed the events since the cave in his mind. He had found a journal of a so-called Psynaut documenting his early life in what, the 1950s or so, and suggesting we're all meant to be Psynauts. Kasya had just run into a Buddhist monk who seemed to know what had happened in the cave already. Kasya thought he must be in a serious Neptune transit, as his astrologer friend would say, for all this to have happened to him at once.

Kasya's first impulse was to run away; the second, to go find Volume 2 of Elbud's journal. But where to look for it? The obvious answer was to follow the monk. So given the urgency of the moment, Kasya ran out of the café after the monk, but he was gone, having disappeared among the hordes of similarly dressed figures in the street.

Kasya needed to regroup, and that meant going back to the familiar. Two days later, he was on a plane back home. But landing at the airport didn't feel like regrouping—it felt like an assault. The noise, the confusion, the advertising, and all the ways his attention was groped for made him feel slightly nauseous, and even more alone and out of touch. Somehow, Kasya felt enslaved. He remembered his friend saying that we have been slowly made into consumer slaves, feudalized into "consumer serf-dom." The richest 1% of the population held 50% of the wealth, that is, about 11 million out of 8 billion people ... out of whack, thought Kasya.

He picked up his luggage and headed off to make connections back home. He was met at the local airport by his family, loaded into the SUV, and driven back to his parent's house since he had sublet his apartment. He exchanged a few pleasantries with them before plopping into bed with exhaustion. The next day was surreal.

After sleeping for almost forever, Kasya took meals with the family. Everyone was talking about their world, and he felt no part of it. Life here was the same as when he had left. He tried to interject a few stories, but his family's interest was insignificant. He did manage to talk about Avalokana and his journal, but that was met by blank stares until his father erupted with, "I don't believe a word of it! And in any case, if it is true, they should all go back to where they came from. Either that, or it's all just a publicity stunt."

Trying to smooth the waters, his mother added, "Anyway, Kasya, it's not so important. You'll find a good career, settle down, raise a family, and forget about all this. Chalk it up to a youthful adventure." With that, she beamed a caring but frozen grin while his dad glowered at his broccoli.

But Kasya knew that wasn't going to work for him. His parents weren't bad people—they just had blinkers on. And his siblings were so engaged with their devices that they might as well have not heard him. Time to move on. He wondered how long he needed to stay to minimize hurting their feelings. Three days wouldn't cut it. A week?

The next day, Kasya visited some friends and tried to fit in with them too. They were marginally more accommodating about listening about his trip to India, but not much more interested than his family had been. When he got to the point in his story about the cave and the journal, they were interrupted by the arrival of his friend's girlfriends, and the conversation went sideways. All their talk was about social media, TV series or movies, jobs, careers, and forging relationships. Kasya joined in as best he could, given he wasn't living in that world.

One young woman, Adana, showed some interest in Kasya, and they saw each other a couple of times over the next week. But one night after making love, he broached his travels and was about to mention the book, and Adana zoned out. Not her thing either, it seemed. He felt like everyone was looking for peace and contentment where it couldn't be found, or wouldn't be permanent. Did Elbud have a Victory Protocol for this? Was it #8, something about struggle?

Kasya felt he was being led down a one-way path, and the second journal was at the end of it. He needed to make some money. Kasya got a job on a construction crew, and given his carpentry skills, managed to make a nice chunk of change in a relatively short period by working overtime. He saved on costs by staying at a friend's apartment and sharing the rent. He spent long hours reading and started to learn how to meditate. Eight months later, he felt he was ready to go looking, but where?

It came as a surprise to Kasya that he had never actually made the decision to go looking or not—he just was! He thought maybe it was the Victory Protocols, which more accurately reflected the world he saw than anything else he could name. They were like fortune cookies: "You will meet a stranger with a message" kind of thing. Or maybe the stories in Avalokana's memoir spoke to him. In any case, as Sherlock said, "The game was afoot."

Remembering Avalokana's last words in the journal, Kasya knew he needed to find a mentor. Three nights later, he had a dream: he was sitting in a class, he couldn't see the teacher, and the sign above the podium said WELCOME TO BRUSSELS. Okay, Brussels was the plan.

He soothed his friends and family, and in spite of their askance looks and questioning attitude, a few days later, Kasya was on a plane over the Atlantic watching a dumb movie and drinking a beer.

***

Upon landing in Belgium, Kasya's first task was finding the Airbnb he had booked online. He had a quick shower and went in search of food—somehow, chicken-or-pasta just hadn't nourished him. Returning to his room, he dropped into bed and slept.

The next day, Kasya found a breakfast place recommended by his host. It was packed, mostly with young people, and there was only one seat at a table in the corner. Kasya asked the guy sitting there if he could join him. He nodded, so Kasya ordered his food at the counter and sat down. While waiting to be served, Kasya exchanged small talk with his table partner. He learned that this guy was going to a lecture given by a Buddhist teacher that evening. Piqued, Kasya asked if he could join, and they arranged to meet that evening. Kasya was starting to freak out by the unlikely probability of all this, but then people win lotteries, don't they?

That evening sitting in the amphitheater, Kasya suddenly remembered seeing an image of this place in a magazine a few weeks earlier. It had been advertising just this event. Feeling slightly let down, Kasya realized his dream had simply been channeling the magazine. Nevertheless, here he was!

The lecturer spoke about basic Buddhist philosophy intermixed with some Christian, Taoist, and Kabbalistic elements as well as the newer, Integral version of spirituality. Afterward, Kasya walked up to the stage to talk with the teacher. He felt like the teacher was looking right through him, as though he could see to his core. It reminded him of that Tibetan monk in the café in Kathmandu. The teacher was a Westerner though, and Black.

Kasya introduced himself, thanked him for the inspiring talk, and mentioned the journal. The teacher, called Bhikkhu Bodhi (aka Isaiah Jordan) froze, gave Kasya a knowing look, and asked him how he found it. Kasya told him honestly.

At this, the Bhikkhu said, "Right, this is the way one progresses through the stages of becoming a Psynaut. The first volume you must find on your own. The second volume must be given to you by a Psynaut. But in order to receive this second volume, you first have to have looked for it by searching for a mentor. The mentor must decide whether the motivation is clear and whether enough effort has been expended to find it. For example, you could indicate that you have an external agreement with the protocols and that you have an inner understanding that making them your own requires effort.

"As for the third volume, the journey changes ... in a way, you write your own book, or someone else does. The route varies from person to person, but whatever path you choose, it will take effort and application."

Kasya made to interject, but the monk put up a hand to stop him.

"You have found me, indicating your effort," he went on. "You have understood the outer expression, as you're looking for more. And now, I have to ask you the questions that determine if you will receive Volume 2. If at this point you are not interested, we can forget about it, and you can move on with your life. If that is the case, please send Volume 1 back to me. On the other hand, if you want to carry on, come see me tomorrow having thought about two questions. One, what is suffering or struggle? Two, can one get free of it and how?

"But first, do you want to continue? This question you must answer right now. Thinking about it will only confuse you."

Without hesitating, Kasya said, "Yes, I want to continue." The immediacy of his answer shocked him. Nonetheless, Kasya thanked the Bhikkhu and made an appointment for the following morning.

The next day, Kasya met the monk. Isaiah asked him if he had thought about the questions, and Kasya responded that he had been up most of the night mulling them over.

Isaiah asked, "Well?"

Kasya paused, drew a breath, and replied, "Suffering is the attachment to people and things that are impermanent, basically everything including one's own thoughts and feelings."

The Bhikkhu nodded and asked, "And is there a release from that?"

Kasya sighed. "I'm not sure, but I'd like to try and find out. It seems to me that release is possible, since so many people, like Jesus and Gautama, have been telling us for so long that it is."

"How?"

"Well, it seems to me that behind our thoughts and feelings, there is a loving, blissful peace ... a silence." Kasya paused and continued, "When things interrupt that peace, we tend to either cling to those things or push them away. Perhaps the pushing away makes for shadow elements, and clinging creates the avoidance of their impermanence, that is, suffering."

Isaiah smiled and handed him Volume 2.

The Victory Protocols

Victory Protocol 1: The greatest value is compassion.

Victory Protocol 2: Only some beings access the methodology to become a Psynaut, although almost all have the capacity.

Victory Protocol 2.1 (variant): Every human being has the potential to access and integrate their Psynaut nature. This has been called Buddha nature, Christ consciousness, God mind, and so on by humans learning the way.

Victory Protocol 3: Karma—or activity, the law of cause and effect—is about choices and their predictable results.

Victory Protocol 3.1 (variant): Karma is forged by the will. The choices we make delineate our path. Our state, therefore, is of our own making, and it can be changed.

Victory Protocol 4: Alaya is part of a supposedly unconsciousness mind wherein impressions of past experiences and karmic actions are stored. From it, our regular consciousness arises and produces all present and future modes of experience in life. When Psynaut awareness is fully realized, the Alaya consciousness is transformed into the mirror-like wisdom, or perfect discrimination.

Victory Protocol 4.1 (variant): The Alaya vijnana, substratum consciousness, refers to the so-called unconscious level of experience. It also includes where our habits are maintained and where they transform. But it is transpersonal; it is everyone's unconscious. It is the essence of consciousness itself.

Victory Protocol 5: There are six bardos, phase changes or in-between states, namely: natural waking, illusory dreaming, altered states, difficult dying, luminous source, and karmic becoming bardo.

Victory Protocol 6: Everything is impermanent, especially the sense of self.

Victory Protocol 7: While reincarnation (building a body) takes time, rebirth (consciousness transference) is instantaneous.

Victory Protocol 8: From the perspective of the ego, life is a struggle.

Victory Protocol 8.1 (variant): Being separated from what is desired is suffering. Being conjoined with what is not desired is also suffering.

Victory Protocol 8.2/18.1 (variants): Suffering occurs because of attachments or aversions generally rooted in greed, hatred, or delusion.

Victory Protocol 8.3 (variant): Life is a struggle.

Victory Protocol 8.4 (variant): Greed = moving towards. Hate = moving against. Confusion = moving away.

Victory Protocol 9: "Rejoice! Your cruel taskmaster, the ego, exists not."

Victory Protocol 9.1 (variant): The sense of a fixed, permanent, independent self is an illusion.

Victory Protocol 9.2 (variant): All things are done for the sake of self.

Victory Protocol 9.3, on self-development (integral): Our self-development as humans tends to follow predictable lines. Step one mixes experiences that develop self-identity with growing cognitive abilities and emerging values as we get older.

Victory Protocol 9.4 (variant): Our values develop through predict-able stages, some of which are: survival, magical thinking, egocentric, absolutist, ambitious, humanistic, global, and unitive.

Victory Protocol 9.5 (variant): Our self-identity develops through predictable stages, some of which are: symbiotic, impulsive, self-protective, conformist, conscientious, and individualistic.

Victory Protocol 9.6 (variant): Views develop in stages, from archaic to mythic to collective to universalist, with various stages in between.

Victory Protocol 9.7 (variant): The ego needs to be constantly reas-sured/affirmed for mental and emotional stability.

Victory Protocol 9.8: Social skills can be learned. But true social skills require seeing through the illusion of a fixed sense of self.

Victory Protocol 10: Life's events gravitate towards and reinforce events of the womb shaping.

Victory Protocol 11: Different levels of meditative absorption are graduated steps for "liftoff" into the realm of Psynaut access. Typically, there are nine such steps.

Victory Protocol 12: Freedom is to abide where there is no abiding.

Victory Protocol 13: Religion is literal; spirituality is metaphorical.

Victory Protocol 14: Four Psynaut realizations: life is a struggle, caused by attachment, release is possible, and there is a methodology of release.

Victory Protocol 15: Four great fears: annihilation, abandonment, mental breakdown (going "crazy"), and being "evil" (the shadow manifesting).

Victory Protocol 16: Our body rides on the energy (chi, wind) contained therein when consciousness embodies. Its movement through the organism's energy centers is called kundalini.

Victory Protocol 17: The birth process initiates all the qualities and strengths we will need to meet life successfully. Interfering with that process creates an enormous struggle.

Victory Protocol 18: Life is a cycle of transformations based on attachments and/or aversions.

Victory Protocol 8.2/18.1 (variants): Suffering occurs because of attachments or aversions generally rooted in greed, hatred, or delusion.

Victory Protocol 19: Emotional states are determined by the human evaluating system known as feelings. Feelings are conditioned by association with what is considered pleasant, unpleasant, or neutral. These two are programmed by previous karma (how the initial contact was delivered and received).

Victory Protocol 20: Generosity is a fundamental element (1 of 6 virtues, more on these later) of a Psynaut's realization. To be generous, we must trust and surrender to the reality that we have enough and can share.

Victory Protocol 20.1 (variant): We train in the six virtues in order to undermine the negative and accentuate the positive, in this case, kind behavior.

Victory Protocol 21: The so-called Psychic powers that arise occasionally, as needed in a Psynaut's work, are not for show.

Victory Protocol 22: Treat all life with respect and disturb it as little as possible.

Victory Protocol 23: We never feel we're ready for the challenge that comes next, but if it is arising, we most probably are.

Victory Protocol 23.1 (variant): What is a challenge for one person is inconsequential for another and vice versa.

Victory Protocol 24: The natural state for a human being is bliss, clarity, and non-clinging.

Victory Protocol 25: We live in a mystery and only see what pops out of the void into our world.

Victory Protocol 26: We are all an interweaving of interdependent patterns, and those patterns trigger a sense of being or person we call "me."

Victory Protocol 27: To realize our Psynaut potential requires training.

Victory Protocol 27.1 (variant): The process of graduating from human to Psynaut involves training that proceeds in steps.

Victory Protocol 28: If you don't rebel, you probably don't meet the Victory Protocols. If you keep rebelling, you probably won't learn them.

Victory Protocol 29: The Mind is nowhere to be found. There is only non-clinging. The mind is transient and insubstantial. There is knowing but no one to know it.

Victory Protocol 30: What measure measures the measurer's measure?

Victory Protocol 31: Desire mind is rooted in human biology. Psynaut mind integrates that and goes beyond it.

Victory Protocol 32: One of the primary elements of a Psynaut's training is joy. (This is one of seven specified elements.)

Victory Protocol 33: Learning to navigate parents prepares us to navigate school, bosses, and spouses.

Victory Protocol 34: Experience plus compassion equals wisdom. Knowledge plus ambition equals selfishness.

Victory Protocol 34.1 (variant): Wisdom is the arrival of dead-end speech.

Victory Protocol 35: Western culture breeds a personal ego; Asian culture breeds a collective ego.

Victory Protocol 36: You are what you hate while you're hating it.

Victory Protocol 37: We see what we believe.

Victory Protocol 38: Most behavior is rooted in habit.

Victory Protocol 39: Prejudice is rooted in making superficial, categorical differences between groups, and devaluing them in comparison to ourselves and our group.

Victory Protocol 40: Recognize the wholesome for the wholesome, and support it to recur (this is one of four efforts.)

Victory Protocol 41: Once you truly understand for yourself why a certain protocol is there, you won't need to keep it; it will keep itself.

Victory Protocol 42: We learn almost everything from someone else. For some things though, like wisdom, it requires a very special teacher.

Victory Protocol 43: Some experiences do not arise until the groundwork has been set in place.

Victory Protocol 44: Time and space are illusions created by the ego to mark its journey.

Victory Protocol 45: The ego takes on an appearance in an attempt to protect from the hurt, and therein lies the trauma.

Victory Protocol 46: Humans tend to dismiss those who don't serve their needs in some immediate fashion.

Victory Protocol 47: A good heart can sometimes support rough behavior if its motivation is pure.

Victory Protocol 48: The ego never feels truly safe because it is an illusion (albeit an unconscious one). Ego is a concept held together by other illusory concepts that makes it seem real.

Victory Protocol 49: A Psynaut is called the good friend, a mentor, an experienced and trusted advisor. Trust starts with love.

Victory Protocol 50: Superior feelings, inferiority complex. Inferior feelings, superiority complex.

Victory Protocol 51: It is often from the "rejected" class that many Psynauts get their start.

Victory Protocol 52: Social intelligence usually means you fit nicely in the middle of the paradigm of your culture.

Victory Protocol 53: Sometimes a small shift in behavior can have significant, unforeseen consequences.

Victory Protocol 54: Your faith shall set you free.

Victory Protocol 55: The shadow aspects of our psyches revolve around the lower three chakras. (See also 9s)

Victory Protocol 56: There are many chakras in the body with different ways to count them. Here we talk of seven. The lower three are roughly at the perineum, the sacral area (lower spine), and solar plexus (abdomen).

Victory Protocol 57: In Buddhism, moral dread and shame are considered wholesome.

Victory Protocol 58: Using sexual intercourse can foster an awakening experience if engaged in with shadow elements in the light.

Victory Protocol 59: When passions and primitive views are in play, virtue declines.

Victory Protocol 60: The eight poisons are fame and shame, loss and gain, praise and blame, pleasure and pain.

Victory Protocol 61: Psychic powers include first and foremost the ability to remain in a clear, blissful, loving state regardless of circumstances.

Victory Protocol 61.1 (variant): Other psychic powers can include the ability to read minds, being able to hear what is not said, recollection of previous lives, knowing other people's karma, and the ability to travel out of body.

Victory Protocol 62: The four obscurations are ignorance, habit, conflicting emotions, and negative actions.

Victory Protocol 63: Four kinds of neuroses can manifest in children stemming from negative shaping: the hurt child, the critical child, the angry child, and the guilty child.

Victory Protocol 64: If you have the responsibility, you must have the authority. If you have the authority, you must be responsible.

Victory Protocol 65: Anger, pride, passion, jealousy, and stupidity are hindrances.

Victory Protocol 66: The question is not "to be or not to be"; the question is "what to be?"

About the Author

Qapel Doug Duncan (July 14, 1949–October 5, 2024) spent his life exploring the vast territories where ancient wisdom meets contemporary understanding—a journey that began with a wandering child in Saskatchewan and culminated in teachings that touched thousands across the globe.

Even as a small boy, Qapel possessed an irrepressible urge to explore beyond known boundaries. Local police became familiar with the young wanderer, often bringing him home from his adventures across the prairies. This early restlessness wasn't mere childhood mischief—it was the first expression of a soul destined to travel far beyond conventional maps, seeking the infinite landscapes of consciousness itself.

In 1974, Qapel encountered Venerable Namgyal Rinpoche, beginning a three-decade apprenticeship that would shape his life's work. Receiving lay ordination in 1978, he became a lineage holder in this distinctive teaching tradition and after decades of intensive study and practice with Namgyal Rinpoche, a rigorous personal practice and numerous solitary retreats,

What set Qapel apart as a teacher wasn't just the breadth of his training, but his remarkable gift for making ancient teachings come alive. Beginning in 1985, he led retreats and training programs from Canada's Arctic to Mongolia, Japan, Bhutan, and Antarctica, weaving together Buddhist philosophy, contemporary psychology, and modern science with an energy and insight that could shake students awake while making them laugh. His teaching style was anything but dry—students remember his infectious enthusiasm, his piercing clarity, and his uncanny ability to meet each person exactly where they were.

In 2005, Qapel co-founded Clear Sky Retreat Center in British Columbia's Rocky Mountains with his partner, Catherine Pawasarat

Sensei, creating a sanctuary where serious practitioners could integrate contemplative wisdom with daily life. There, nestled among ancient mountains, he continued teaching until his passing in October 2024, his presence a living bridge between the ordinary and the extraordinary.

Psynauts represents Qapel's singular venture into fiction—a departure from his previous dharma books, yet perhaps his most complete teaching. In this three-volume series, he channels decades of spiritual insight into an engaging narrative that explores consciousness, awakening, and humanity's cosmic potential. Here, the restless wanderer from Saskatchewan offers his final gift: a story that reminds us the greatest adventures happen not in distant lands, but in the courageous journey of ordinary people awakening to our true nature.

Those who knew Qapel remember not just a teacher of profound wisdom, but a warm, energetic presence who could be simultaneously playful and piercing, gentle and uncompromising. He lived what he taught—that freedom from suffering is possible, that awakening is our birthright, and that the path itself is filled with joy.

In *Psynauts*, readers will recognize that characteristic blend: the rigorous insight of a master teacher wrapped in humor and adventure, and the profound compassion of someone who genuinely walked the path he described.

Learn more about Qapel's teachings at planetdharma.com and Clear Sky Retreat Center at clearskycenter.org.